below.

SPECIAL MESSAGE TO READERS

THE ULVERSCROFT FOUNDATION
(registered UK charity number 264873)
was established in 1972 to provide funds for
research, diagnosis and treatment of eye diseases.
Examples of major projects funded by
the Ulverscroft Foundation are:-

- The Children's Eye Unit at Moorfields Eye
  Hospital, London
- The Ulverscroft Children's Eye Unit at Great
  Ormond Street Hospital for Sick Children
- Funding research into eye diseases and
  treatment at the Department of Ophthalmology,
  University of Leicester
- The Ulverscroft Vision Research Group,
  Institute of Child Health
- Twin operating theatres at the Western
  Ophthalmic Hospital, London
- The Chair of Ophthalmology at the Royal
  Australian College of Ophthalmologists

You can help further the work of the Foundation
by making a donation or leaving a legacy.
Every contribution is gratefully received. If you
would like to help support the Foundation or
require further information, please contact:

THE ULVERSCROFT FOUNDATION
The Green, Bradgate Road, Anstey
Leicester LE7 7FU, England
Tel: (0116) 236 4325
website: www.foundation.ulverscroft.com

THE SUBSTANCE OF A SHADE

Soon after moving into Mexton Grange, an old Georgian country house in the Cotswolds, Alice hears disquieting stories and rumours about her new abode: the previous owners had been driven out by a strange, oppressive atmosphere in the house. It was not as if the house was *actually* haunted — rather, it was as if the house was *waiting to be haunted* . . . These five stories of terror and the macabre by John Glasby will tingle the spine on any dark and stormy night.

Books by John Glasby
in the Linford Mystery Library:

THE SAVAGE CITY
A TIME FOR MURDER
DEATH NEVER STRIKES TWICE
THE DARK DESTROYER
DARK CONFLICT
THE UNDEAD
DEATH COMES CALLING
MURDER IS MY SHADOW
DARK LEGION
THE WHEEL SPINS THIRTEEN
MYSTERY OF THE CRATER
ROSES FOR A LADY
PROJECT JOVE
THE MISSING HEIRESS MURDERS
THE DARK BOATMAN
THE LONELY SHADOWS

NORTHUMBERLAND

022044494

Accession No.

F

Class No.

COUNTY LIBRARY

JOHN GLASBY

THE SUBSTANCE OF A SHADE & OTHER STORIES

Complete and Unabridged

LINFORD
Leicester

First published in Great Britain

First Linford Edition
published 2014

Copyright © 2003 by John Glasby
Copyright © 2013 by the Estate of John Glasby
All rights reserved

A catalogue record for this book is available
from the British Library.

ISBN 978–1–4448–1977–9

Published by
F. A. Thorpe (Publishing)
Anstey, Leicestershire

Set by Words & Graphics Ltd.
Anstey, Leicestershire
Printed and bound in Great Britain by
T. J. International Ltd., Padstow, Cornwall

This book is printed on acid-free paper

THE SUBSTANCE OF
A SHADE

When Alice Merdon bought Mexton Grange there was not the slightest hint of anything abnormal about the house. Indeed, viewing it for the first time in late autumn sunlight, it had looked the ideal spot where her brother, Stephen, might recuperate and return to something like his former self. A charming Georgian house with a high-walled garden, it stood alone perhaps half a mile from Framford, a tiny village in the heart of the Cotswolds.

Since the horrible car accident six months earlier, she had looked after her brother, struggling to come to terms with the fact that he no longer really knew her. The doctors had told her that amnesia was a not uncommon outcome of such injuries, that Stephen was extremely lucky to be alive, and although not promising anything, there was a good chance he

1

would regain his memory in time.

Yet if the truth were known, there was something about Stephen's condition which troubled her more than the amnesia. In spite of all her enquiries, Alice had learned very little of the actual details of the accident beyond the fact that no other vehicle had been involved. The road and weather conditions had been excellent at the time, yet for some unaccountable reason his car had gone out of control, veered across the road, and plunged three hundred feet down a precipitous slope.

What had happened thereafter was something of a mystery. By the time the emergency services had arrived on the scene, the car was a burnt-out wreck, yet her brother had been discovered, virtually unscathed, wandering in a dazed condition a short distance away, his mind a total blank. She had visited him in hospital where he had been taken for observation and had listened to the doctors describe his escape as little short of miraculous. Stephen had suffered nothing more than a blow to the head

2

and a few abrasions and their only conclusion was that, somehow, he had been thrown clear of the car moments before the impact. The other passenger in the vehicle, however, had not been so fortunate, having perished in the flames when the ruptured petrol tank had exploded. So far, despite numerous inquiries, the police had come up with no clue to his identity. If he had been an acquaintance of Stephen's, his name was still locked away somewhere in his mind, shut off from his consciousness.

On his release from hospital, Alice had taken him back to the house on the outskirts of London, hoping that their once-familiar surroundings might prompt him to remember his past life. Yet from the first she had detected something strange in his manner as if, at times, he was utterly oblivious to his surroundings, existing in some private world where nothing could enter.

Initially, she had put this down to the accident, to his inability to recall any event that occurred prior to the car veering off the road.

He seldom ventured out beyond the house and small garden and Alice would often find him staring into the large, full-length mirror which stood in the hall, peering intently at his reflection. When she had mentioned this to the doctor, however, the latter merely said that such idiosyncrasies were to be expected in cases of total amnesia and it was nothing for her to worry about. But Alice did worry and after a time, when it became clear that his condition was showing no sign of improvement, she decided it might be best if they were to move from London to a more peaceful and secluded spot in the country.

Neither of them had married, both were in their fifties and relatively well-off, so moving presented no financial difficulties. There was nothing to keep them in town and it was possible that living in the country might prove beneficial to them both. Once events were set in motion, for Alice was a very determined woman, they swiftly reached the desired conclusion. By mid-October, all the details had been settled, certain necessary renovations had been completed to her satisfaction and, on a crisp, sunny morning, they drove through the pleasant countryside to Framford. Here, they stopped to visit Mr. Blandwell, the estate agent with whom Alice had dealt, in order to pick up the keys to the Grange.

'I trust you'll find everything to your satisfaction, Miss Merdon,' Blandwell said. 'Since you left most of the details to me, I've already inspected the work which had to be carried out and I'm sure once you see it, you will agree everything has been done as you wished. I've also made inquiries in the village should you require any daily help. Of course, being a very large house with extensive grounds, you may find it difficult to manage it all by yourself.'

'Perhaps a housekeeper and gardener would be sufficient until we've settled in,' Alice replied. She eyed the estate agent speculatively, detecting something in his manner that seemed a little out of place. He appeared oddly nervous, as if there was something he wished to impart but he was uncertain how to broach the subject.

'I'm sure that can be arranged.' Blandwell fiddled with his pen for a moment. Then, noticing her watching him curiously, he laid it down on the desk in front of him. After a pause, he continued: 'Normally, with a big house such as the Grange, the servants would live in, but — '

'There's something odd about the Grange; is that what you're trying to say?'

Blandwell looked momentarily flustered, caught off-guard, taking up his pen again to cover his obvious confusion. Swallowing, he said hesitantly: 'There is some talk, of course. But in a small community such as this, such things are to be expected.'

Alice stifled a faint shudder, coupled with a rising anger. Was this man trying to tell them that Mexton Grange was haunted? If so, she should have been told of this before. She, herself, did not believe in ghosts, or anything to do with the supernatural. But Stephen might be another matter. She had bought the Grange in the hope that the peace and tranquility of the countryside might bring back his memory and improve his general health. What traumatic effect might such non-sensical stories have on someone who had had such a close brush with death?

'May I inquire what kind of stories these are?' she asked tartly.

Blandwell spread his hands in a gesture that meant to imply that he did not believe any of them. 'Oh, the Grange isn't haunted; not in the usual sense, anyway.' He forced a quick laugh. 'There are no ghosts prowling the rooms and corridors, no rattling of chains at dead of night. Just — ' He paused abruptly, finding it difficult to put his thoughts into words.

'Go on,' Alice insisted, leaning forward a little in her chair. She wished she had left Stephen in the car and come up here alone for the keys. A quick, sideways glance at her brother, however, showed her that his face still bore his usual bored expression. He seemed to have withdrawn into his private world and was taking no interest in the proceedings.

Blandwell placed the tips of his fingers together and regarded her solemnly over the fleshy pyramid. 'I've no doubt you'll hear some of these tales yourself, Miss Merdon, all I can tell you is what I heard from the previous owner, a Yorkshire businessman named Galworthy. He and his family lived there for six years before returning north. Apparently, it was the atmosphere inside the place that struck him as distinctly unusual — as if the house was waiting to be haunted. Those were his exact words.'

'Waiting to be haunted?' Alice repeated. 'What an odd expression.'

'Indeed,' Blandwell agreed. His voice resumed a little of its former briskness. 'But as you can see, there is nothing of which to be afraid in Mexton Grange. As I've said, the former owner lived there for six years and, apart from this odd atmosphere, he saw and heard nothing. I believe we can safely assume it was nothing more than imagination.'

'I sincerely hope so.' Nodding curtly, Alice took the proffered keys and rose from her chair, motioning to her brother to do likewise. 'We came here from London in search of peace and quiet.'

'And I'm sure you'll find them here.'

The estate agent forced a broad smile as he shook hands. 'You strike me as a down-to-earth woman, Miss Merdon. Take my advice; ignore all of the village gossip and I'm sure you'll both be very happy here.'

* * *

With Stephen seated silently beside her, Alice turned the car off the narrow country lane and passed through the large ornate gates into the wide drive. A row of slender beeches hid the house from view until they turned a curve in the drive. Here there were well-kept lawns and flower borders with a stone fountain in the middle, throwing a cascade of glittering drops high into the still air.

The day was unusually mild for the time of year and in the warm sunlight the house looked particularly attractive with the tall gables on either side of the front door. Parking the car, she got out, waited for Stephen, then climbed the stone steps between twin carved lions which stared sightlessly across the lawn. Unlocking the door, she led the way inside.

Their furniture had been brought in two days earlier and they had stayed at a hotel for the past couple of nights. Now, in the streaming sunlight pouring in through the wide windows, it seemed pathetically little in the great hallways and massive rooms with their high vaulted ceilings. Alice felt a sudden qualm of misgiving, emerging from she knew not what secret part of her mind.

There *was* a certain peculiar atmosphere inside the house. Yet she could not analyse it. It was not exactly a creepy sensation; rather it was an air of malignant expectancy — as if the place was waiting for something terrible to happen. It was strange she had not experienced it on that earlier occasion when she had been shown around the Grange.

She fought down the tiny shiver and for the remainder of the day busied herself in arranging things to her taste and exploring the numerous rooms. Stephen accompanied her at times, occasionally showing a spark of interest in the older parts of the house. Prior to his accident, he had been a prominent architect and this had been one of the reasons for her choosing this place, possessing as it did many unique architectural features.

That night she found it difficult to fall asleep. Her bedroom was adjacent to Stephen's at the rear of the house and, although she could not hear him moving around, she knew intuitively that he was still awake. The odd creaks and groans of the ancient timbers kept intruding into her thoughts. An occasional thumping from the basement also kept sleep at bay even though she knew this was due to the boiler, which still required servicing. But these were normal sounds; the kind to be expected in such an old building.

After a time, she realised that what she was really straining to pick out, what was really keeping her awake and in such a curious state of tension, were sounds she could not hear, something that lay concealed behind the ordinary noises.

Eventually she must have fallen into an uneasy doze for when she woke, jerking upright in the large bed, it was still dark. At first, she could not determine what had woken her. The house was very still; even sounds she had previously heard were absent. Outside, there was not a breath of wind.

Through the window, she could clearly make out the topmost branches of the distant trees in the flooding yellow moonlight. They were absolutely motionless. Not a leaf stirred and it was if the entire world was static, holding its breath and waiting for something to happen. She knew quite well how fantastic such an idea was, but it was impossible to get it out of her mind.

Could it have been simply the onset of this sudden silence that had woken her, she wondered; just as the abrupt stopping of a ticking clock could do? The notion flashed quickly through her thoughts but then, an instant later, she picked out the soft sounds of footsteps passing her door. For a moment her heart leapt, hammering wildly, into her throat. Then she forced herself to think clearly. She had forgotten how restless Stephen normally was, recalling his nocturnal perambulations through their London home in the early hours of the morning. He had never been a good sleeper but this unrest had become more pronounced following his accident.

Yet curiously, she had not heard his bedroom door open and close and earlier she had noticed how almost all the doors needed oiling, creaking loudly whenever she had pulled them open during her exploration of the rooms. But if it were not her brother, who on earth could it be? Easing herself out of bed, she slipped into her robe and moved hesitantly to the door. Trembling a little, she threw the door open. The corridor outside was empty but she could still hear the footsteps ascending the stairway at the end of the corridor. In spite of the warm robe, Alice felt as if a blast of icy air had momentarily swept through the house. This is ridiculous, she told herself fiercely. There are no such things as ghosts — and as for that stupid tale she had heard from the estate agent, that was nothing more than imagination and idle village gossip.

Pulling the robe more tightly around her thin body, she moved to the end of the passage. Here, there was a second flight of stairs, narrower than the others, leading to the top of the house. A long shaft of bright moonlight streamed through the semi-circular window high on the wall, illuminating stairs. There was no one there although for a second she thought she glimpsed a dark shadow across the very top. But she had caught it with averted vision and the instant she stared directly at it, it disappeared and she could not be certain there had been anyone there at all.

But those footsteps had been real. Clutching at the wall, she leaned against it, listening to the silence, waiting for some sound to break the stillness.

None came.

The house was as silent as the grave.

Allowing her pent-up breath to escape in a long sigh, she started up the stairs. Her entire system had been prodded into awareness by the sound, her tiredness forgotten. At the top of the stairs, a wide corridor stretched away in front of her, running almost the entire length of the building. Here, the rooms were all empty.

The amount of furniture they had brought with them from London was far too inadequate to fill all of this huge place and for the time being she decided to leave them as they were.

At the far end of the corridor, a large window overlooked the side gardens but halfway along the passage a swathe of moonlight shone through an open door. Frowning, her heart palpitating a little with a tiny germ of panic, she remembered she had closed all of the doors on this floor that afternoon. Cautiously, she edged towards the room and peered through the open door. A wave of relief washed through her. Stephen stood in the middle of the room staring blankly around him.

Going forward, she took his arm gently. His eyes were now staring straight ahead of him and her first thought was that he must be sleepwalking.

'Come along, Stephen,' she said quietly. 'I'll take you back to bed.'

For a moment, he gazed at her with no sign of recognition. Then his lips moved as he forced the words out. 'I heard someone calling me,' he mumbled. 'Someone in this house.'

'Nonsense. There is no one here,' she replied reassuringly. 'You must have been dreaming. Now let's get you back to bed. You'll catch your death of cold wandering around at this time of night.'

Without resisting, he allowed her to lead him out of the room. There was an odd lost expression on his face and his head was cocked a little on one side as if listening for small sounds that only he could hear.

Guiding him back to his room, she waited until he slid into bed, then pulled the covers over his chest. 'I did hear something,' he insisted.

'You just imagined you did,' she told him fiercely. 'This is our first night in a new house and it will take some time getting used to. But there's nothing here.' Straightening up, she added: 'Now try to get some sleep. You'll feel a lot better in the morning.'

★　★　★

When Stephen came down to breakfast the next morning, it was clear to Alice that he had not slept well. There were dark circles under his eyes and his movements were characterised by the same listlessness she had noticed the night before. He ate his food mechanically as if it were something which had to be done but which he did not relish. At intervals, he would lift his head to peer around the room in an attitude of listening.

When this happened for the fourth or fifth time, she asked: 'Do you still hear it, Stephen?'

'What?' Her voice seemed to make him jump nervously. Then he recovered his composure with an effort. 'No, I — '

'Last night, you went up into one the rooms at the top of the house and when I found you, you told me that someone was calling to you.'

'Did I?' Stephen looked perplexed. 'I don't remember.'

'I thought you might be walking in your sleep,' Alice went on. She finished her toast and sat back, determined to get to the bottom of what was happening. 'But you were wide awake and, apart from this foolish notion of someone in the house, quite rational. Now, try to remember what happened.'

Stephen rubbed a hand across his forehead. He sat quite still, struggling to remember.

Prompting him, Alice said: 'Were you awake all that time after going to your room? Or did you sleep and someone woke you?' She expressed a faint qualm of unease, like a tight knot in her stomach. She had to come to terms with the amnesia brought on by the accident. But was his more recent memory fading?

'I . . . I remember waking so I must have slept for a while,' Stephen began hesitantly. 'It was from a strange dream. I can't recall much of it but there were voices telling me I had to go somewhere but I had no idea where it was they wanted me to go. I know it had something to do with this house.'

'Is that why you went up to that particular room?'

'I suppose it must have been. I know this may sound odd, as if I'm losing my mind, but those voices were still there after I woke up. I could hear them whispering to me and there was one voice, louder and more insistent than the others, telling me I had no right to be here.'

'Well, I certainly heard nothing. So it must have been your imagination,' Alice declared. She decided to let the matter drop there for it was clear there was nothing more he could tell her.

As the day went on, however, she found herself watching him more closely, sometimes listening herself. But there were no sounds that had no right to be present. If this continued, or if Stephen's condition worsened, she would have to consult the local doctor.

In the afternoon she decided to take a walk in the village. They had brought only a little food with them and were almost out of certain items. She could have taken the car but it was such a beautiful day and the fresh air might help to clear her of the morbid thoughts that were plaguing her. Entering the small square half an hour later, she found the grocery store crushed between 'The Green Man' inn and a hardware shop. A bell jangled noisily as she opened the door and stepped inside.

Consulting the list she had brought with her, she made her way around the shelves, acutely aware that the elderly woman behind the counter was watching her with open curiosity. Taking the basket to the counter, Alice waited patiently while the woman totalled her purchases.

'You're the new owner of the Grange, aren't you?'

'That's right,' Alice said, slipping her change into her purse. 'We moved in yesterday.'

'I thought I recognised you. I saw you leaving Mr. Blandwell's office. I hope you'll be happy there.'

Alice turned to leave, then paused. There was no one else in the shop and it was possible she might learn a little more about Mexton Grange.

'Did you know the last owner?' she asked.

'Mr. Galworthy? Why, yes. I knew him, and his family, well. They lived here for several years and were well known, and liked, in the village. The children used to come in quite often to see me.'

'Did he ever mention there was — ' Alice struggled to find the right words, ' — anything peculiar about the house?' she finished lamely.

'Peculiar? Why, no, not to my knowledge. It's very old, of course, but if you're suggesting it might be haunted, I wouldn't believe that for one minute.'

'Perhaps I'm just being over-imaginative.' Alice gave a little laugh. 'It's just something Mr. Blandwell said that set me wondering.'

'Well, all I can say is I've lived in Framford all my life and I've never heard anything.' As Alice reached the door, the shopkeeper said: 'If you're worried about anything connected with the house, you'd best talk with the vicar. He and Mr. Galworthy became firm friends and if there is anything strange, I'm sure he'll be able to help you.'

'Thank you.'

Leaving the shop, Alice made her way slowly along the narrow street. On the outskirts of the village, where the road ran on between the fields where the corn stubble from the recent harvest stood up like brown bristles from the soil, she passed the ancient church with its Norman tower and time-mellowed walls. It was just as she walked past the gate leading into the churchyard that she spotted the tall gaunt figure coming towards her from the porch. She had not intended to seek out the vicar that afternoon, yet there was no doubt in her mind that this was the man the shopkeeper had spoken of and some sudden impulse caused her to stop and wait until the clergyman reached the gate.

The man who came out was older than she had expected. Now that she saw him clearly she realised he must be well into his seventies, well after the age she thought men of the cloth retired.

'You'll be Miss Merdon.' The vicar extended his hand. 'My name is Walters, the vicar of this little parish.'

Alice looked momentarily surprised.

Smiling, the vicar went on: 'News travels fast in a small community like Framford. I guessed that the Grange had new owners when I noticed all the renovations taking place. As to knowing your name, Arnold Blandwell is an old friend and one of the pillars of our church.'

Alice gave an uncertain smile. 'I was meaning to visit you sometime,' she said. 'I understand you know a lot about the village and particularly Mexton Grange and — '

Looking at him, she guessed with a measure of certainty what was in his mind when he said: 'What better time than now? Unless, of course, you're in a hurry to get back. We can talk at the rectory.'

For a moment, she hesitated then accepted his offer, falling into step behind him as he led the way along the road, then turned in through a large gate.

The rectory was set back from the road at the end of a red gravel drive. Although dating from some time in the middle of the last century, it looked modern in contrast to the ancient church itself.

Five minutes later Alice was seated in a comfortable armchair in the vicar's parlour. The massive oak desk in front of her, behind which Walters had seated himself, was evidently that at which he wrote his Sunday sermons for it was covered with books and sheets of paper.

Once the maid had brought tea, Walters said solemnly: 'I gather you wish to see me on matters concerning the Grange and, perhaps, its previous owner.'

Alison glanced up quickly from her cup, startled by her host's uncanny insight.

'That's true,' she admitted. 'But how —?'

Walters smiled faintly. 'It was more an intuitive conclusion than a guess, Miss Merdon. Had you merely wished to introduce yourself, you would almost certainly have done that after church next Sunday. I feel, therefore, that you have something of a more serious nature on your mind.'

Alice sipped her tea for a moment, trying to form her thoughts into words. When looked at objectively, it all seemed so silly. Yet there could be no denying she had felt that peculiar atmosphere immediately on setting foot inside the house.

As if understanding her difficulty, Walters said gravely: 'Have you been told anything in the village? Or perhaps you've felt something in the house?'

With an effort, Alice forced her thoughts into rational channels. 'Both,' she replied firmly. 'I was told something by the estate agent of what the last owner had said and I must admit I get the most uncomfortable feeling at times inside the house. But I'm not worried for myself. I'm more vexed about the effect this may have on my brother.'

'Your brother?' Walters asked. For a second, a strange expression flitted across his lined features.

Nodding, Alice gave him a brief account of the accident and Stephen's subsequent amnesia, concluding with the odd incident of the previous night.

Walters listened attentively, not interrupting once. When she had finished, he remained silent for a full minute. Then, leaning forward, and resting his elbows on the desk, he said solemnly: 'I can understand your concern, Miss Merdon. But I assure you it's completely groundless. I believe I can justifiably say I know more about Mexton Grange than anyone else in the village. I've lived here all of my life and I can state, quite categorically, that the Grange is not haunted.'

Alice made to interrupt but he held up one hand to stop her. 'I know that most places as old as the Grange have certain ghostly reputations, possibly with some justification. However, the history of Mexton Grange, and those who have lived there since it was built, has been extremely uneventful. There have been no murders, suicides, or mysterious deaths which might give rise to ghostly manifestations.'

'But this peculiar atmosphere inside the house,' Alice protested.

'There've been rumours, of course,' Walters admitted. He tapped absently on the desk with his forefinger.

'Can you be more explicit, vicar?' Alice asked. 'Personally, I don't believe in ghosts. The dead stay dead. But my concern is with my brother, how this might affect him.'

'I quite understand your position. Unfortunately, I don't see how I can help you any further except to say that should anything out of the ordinary happen, you can always come to me for help.' Walters paused as if a sudden thought had struck him. 'I do recall one strange thing, however. Unlike her husband, Evelyn Galworthy was a very religious woman, never missed a Sunday service although he seldom attended church. We had a garden fête one day as I remember, shortly after they had moved into the house. Naturally, I asked how she liked the Grange and she said a very odd thing. She said that there were times when she had the feeling she was living in limbo.'

'Did you ask her what she meant by that?'

'Yes.' Walters nodded. 'She said that was the only way she could describe it; as if the house was a place for lost souls waiting to go on to a higher plane. Exactly as we believe in the church.'

'How peculiar.' Despite her previous disbeliefs, Alison experienced a sudden chill. 'Yet you say there is no history of any hauntings.'

'None at all. Had there been, it would certainly have become public knowledge long before now. People who live in a small isolated community such as this almost always turn out to be highly superstitious.'

Leaving the rectory, Alice made her way back to the Grange, pondering deeply on what the vicar had told her. Certainly, much of what he had said tallied with the estate agent's outspoken comments and, she realised abruptly, with her own feelings. There *was* a peculiar waiting quality about the house. If it had happened only to herself and Stephen she might have put it down to imagination, or living in such an isolated spot after living all their lives in the city. But, clearly, others had felt it too.

Letting herself into the house, she called Stephen's name. When there was no answer, she shouted again, more loudly, before running upstairs. Her anxiety grew when she could find no trace of him. Then, entering the room at the top where she had found him the previous night, she happened to glance through the window.

Her initial sense of relief at seeing him standing in the garden below was instantly replaced by one of apprehension. He was standing absolutely still beside one of the flowerbeds in exactly the same attitude of listening as she had found him earlier. Hurrying downstairs, she ran outside and around the corner of the building. Again, she called his name but he gave no indication that he heard her. Not until she came right up to him did he turn his head to look at her.

'You gave me quite a fright,' she said, a trifle more sharply than she had intended. 'I thought you would stay inside.' She experienced a little tremor of anxiety at the vacant, faraway look in his eyes.

'I'm sorry. I just had to get out, away from those voices.'

Swallowing hard, Alice forced herself to keep a tight control on her emotions. Despite the vicar's assurances, she was certain there was something about this place which was definitely unwholesome. Forcing calmness into her voice, she said: 'Do you hear those voices all the time, Stephen? Can you tell me what they are saying?'

Stephen put a hand up to his forehead. 'They're mostly just whispers, sometimes so faint I can hardly hear them. It's difficult to make out any words but I get the feeling they're telling me I can't stay here.'

Very gently, Alice said: 'I don't hear anything, Stephen. The doctor said you might have odd symptoms but these are all due to the accident, nothing more. And certainly nothing to do with the house. It may just be that — '

'That knock on the head caused more than a simple concussion,' Stephen interrupted harshly. 'I know what they said. They assured me there was no permanent damage to the brain and that, perhaps, in time my memory would return. But what do they know? If I start hearing things which aren't there, that's a sure sign of madness, isn't it?'

'Certainly not!' Alice retorted vehemently. 'You're no more insane than I am. First thing in the morning, we'll drive into the village and get the doctor to give you a complete check-up. I'm sure there's a logical explanation for this.'

Once inside the house, she busied herself preparing a meal, leaving Stephen sitting in the chair in front of the fire. She refused to believe that her brother was going insane, telling herself that this odd episode might be a common occurrence to people who had received a violent blow to the head. Not only that, she realised, but there had been no intimation of this curious behaviour before they had come to the Grange. All the time they had stayed in London there had been only the amnesia troubling him. No whispering voices in his mind telling him he didn't belong.

So it had to be this house that had sparked off this odd visitation. Perhaps, for some reason, he had taken an instant dislike to it and this aversion had manifested itself in this form. His mind was still not completely rational and this was his way of telling himself that the house rejected him. Once that thought had entered her mind, Alice clung to it desperately. It was a plausible explanation and she would discuss it at length with the doctor the next day.

That night, she lay awake in her bed for two hours, listening for the faint sound to indicate that Stephen might leave his room.

But there was nothing and she finally fell into a deep sleep. When she woke the sun was streaming in through the window and glancing at the clock on her bedside table, she saw it was almost eight-thirty. Dressing hurriedly, she went out and knocked loudly on Stephen's door.

When there was no answer, she thrust it open and peered inside. His bed had been slept in but there was no sign of him. Running downstairs, she found him in the hall, standing in front of the long mirror, staring intently into the glass.

'What on earth are you doing, Stephen?' she asked. 'Is there anything wrong?'

He jumped nervously at the sound of her voice. 'It's nothing,' he said, a note of confusion in his tone. 'I thought I saw something reflected in the glass just as I made to walk past.'

Alice stood beside him, trembling a little. She saw nothing out of the ordinary; just two figures of Stephen and herself with the opposite wall in the background. Then, just for an instant, it seemed that the glass reflection was oddly distorted. The effect was so transient that she could not be absolutely certain that she saw anything at all.

Yet there had been something. A brief movement as if part of the glass had rippled, rather like those mirrors in the amusement arcades, which greatly warped one's image. It had been only momentary and the impression had only affected Stephen's image, causing it to quiver strangely.

Shaking her head a little to clear it of the curious thoughts passing through her mind, she took her brother's arm and led him into the dining room. Inwardly, she felt troubled, but she was determined not to show it. She knew Stephen had been lying when he had claimed he was merely passing the mirror. She had picked out no sound of movement when coming down the stairs and was convinced he had been standing there for a long time.

During breakfast, they spoke little. As always now, he ate his food with an involuntary abstractness as if he was scarcely aware of his actions. Watching him covertly, she had no doubt that his being in this house was having an adverse effect upon his general attitude, which disturbed her.

It was not until she was in the kitchen, washing up the breakfast dishes, that it came to her in a sudden flash of clarity.

Just like the house, Stephen gave the unmistakable impression of waiting for something, which would inevitably happen: something dreadful that lay in the not too distant future!

Was it possible there was some maleficent influence associated with this place and, for some reason, it had transferred itself to him? Wiping her hands on the towel, she went back to stand in the doorway, looking into the room where Stephen stood with his back to the wide stone hearth, his hands clasped behind him.

'I've made up my mind, Stephen,' she said firmly. 'I'm taking you to the village to see the doctor.' When he made to argue, she cut him off quickly. 'Now no arguments. This is for my peace of mind as well of your own. There is something troubling you and the sooner we get to the bottom of it, the better.'

She expected him to make further objections to her suggestion but instead, he merely shrugged his shoulders as if it mattered little to him whether they went or not.

Accordingly, at ten o'clock, they left the Grange with Stephen sitting silent in the passenger seat, apparently taking no interest in what was happening. Parking the car in one corner of the quiet square, Alice got out and went on to the small grocery store to ask directions to the doctor's surgery. The shopkeeper accompanied her back to the door, giving directions. 'There's no call for Dr. Tremayne to have a regular surgery,' she explained. 'He sees all of his patients in the house. You'll find it quite easily. Just take the first turning on the left and it's right at the far end of the lane.'

Thanking her, Alice returned to Stephen and accompanied him along the lane where they found the house at the end with the doctor's name, Andrew Tremayne, on the brass plate near the door.

There was no one waiting in the small outer room and they were shown immediately into a larger room that clearly served as his surgery. Dr. Tremayne was a small, grey-haired man in his late fifties with a trim moustache and piercing blue eyes which surveyed them both with an appraising look as he motioned them to the chairs in front of his desk. He looked a little puzzled seeing both of them together.

'What seems to be the trouble, Mrs. — ?'

'Miss Merdon,' Alice corrected him. 'This is my brother, Stephen. We have only just moved into the Grange and — '

'Ah, yes.' The doctor nodded. 'I heard you were moving in. But I didn't expect to see you so soon.' He leaned back in his chair, placing the tips of his fingers together. 'You both wish to be put on my list?'

'Yes, of course. But I'd also like you to examine my brother. He was recently involved in a car accident which caused total amnesia.'

Tremayne pursed his lips and allowed his glance to stray back to Stephen. 'I presume you've already been thoroughly examined.'

'I spent two weeks in hospital,' Stephen replied hesitantly. 'Since then, my doctor in London has also seen me.'

'And you can remember nothing of what happened in your life prior to the accident?'

'Nothing.' Stephen shook his head slowly. He seemed to have some difficulty focusing on the doctor.

'From what we have been told, he was thrown clear of the car just before it hit the bottom of the ravine and burst into flames,' Alice interrupted. 'Apparently, he had few external injuries beyond some abrasions and concussion. However, he can remember only what's happened since then. But that isn't the reason I'd like you to examine him.'

Tremayne leaned forward and rested his weight on his elbows, looking directly at her. He said nothing, waiting for her to continue.

'We've only been in the Grange for two days, doctor,' she began. 'But something strange seems to be happening to him, something I don't understand. He keeps hearing voices telling him he doesn't belong there. The first night I found him in one of the rooms upstairs and I don't think he really knows how he got there.'

'Do you hear anything?'

Momentarily, Alice was taken aback by the doctor's question. Then she shook her head vehemently. 'Certainly not. How could I? There are only two of us in the house. No one else.'

'I see.'

'I must admit there's something odd about the place, an eerie feeling I sensed the moment we moved in.'

'Perhaps if you could describe this feeling for me. Old houses often possess some kind of aura which certain sensitive people can detect, whereas others are not affected at all.'

'It's as if — ' Alice tried to find the right words, ' — as if the house is waiting for something. There's nothing there at the moment, no ghosts or anything like that, but there is a sensation that it's lying in wait for something to happen very soon.'

'Hmm.' Dr. Tremayne tapped his teeth with his pen, and scribbled something on the pad in front of him. 'Very well. I'll certainly give you a physical check-up, Mr. Merdon.' Turning to Alice, he added: 'But if this is a mental condition, as it may well be, I'm afraid it's a little out of my province. If you'd just wait outside while I examine your brother.'

Alice made to protest, then submitted gracefully. She realised she was giving the impression that Stephen was unable to act and think for himself, but he now seemed so helpless, so uncaring of what went on around him, that she felt she had to act in this way. Going out, she seated herself in one of the chairs against the wall. Picking up a magazine from the small table, she tried to read. But it was impossible. The words seemed to dance tantalisingly in front of her vision and she could not concentrate. Inwardly, she recognised that she was already fearing the worst.

Somehow, that blow on the head had not only affected Stephen's memory; it was also affecting his sanity. Certainly, it had been a mistake to bring him to Mexton Grange. Whatever strange influence lay within that house, it was having a traumatic effect on him. She had never believed in the occult or anything to do with the supernatural before but now, for the first time in her life, she was beginning to think there might be forces in the world which were, for the most part, beyond normal human knowledge.

Ten minutes later, the door opened and Stephen came in, buttoning his jacket. His face was just as expressionless as ever. Dr. Tremayne followed him. He beckoned to Alice.

When they were inside his surgery with the door closed behind them, he said gravely: 'I've given your brother a thorough physical examination. I can assure you there is nothing organically wrong with him apart from one curious thing.'

'What's that?' Alice asked nervously.

'His heartbeat is perfectly regular as far as I can determine, yet so faint I could only just pick it up. It might be nothing, of course. But I would like to see him again in a couple of weeks. As for his mental condition that's a different matter. Apart from his amnesia, which is quite common following such accidents, has he ever mentioned hearing voices before you came to live at the Grange?'

'Never,' Alice replied emphatically. 'I'm

sure he would have told me of anything like that.'

'I see.' Tremayne paused for a moment, studying her seriously over his spectacles. 'Then, at the moment, I can only conclude that the two are linked in some way. You know, of course, that there have been some queer rumours concerning the Grange over the past few years.'

'I've been told certain things,' Alice admitted. 'Not that I believe in any of them. I've been assured the place isn't haunted. But if there is something about that house which is having this adverse effect on him, I'd like to know about it.'

Tremayne sighed audibly. 'I only wish I could help you there. But I'm just an ordinary country doctor and these things are better treated by specialists. Your brother seems oddly reticent about talking of these voices he hears. My first impression is that he doesn't like to discuss them because I may think he's going mad.'

'I don't quite follow you, doctor.'

'I think, deep down, he knows what these voices are, and what they're telling him.'

Alice shook her head in a bewildered way. She realised her hands were shaking as she gripped the sides of the chair convulsively. Deliberately, she forced herself to relax. 'Do you think he's going insane?' she asked bluntly.

'No, I'm quite sure that's not the case. This is something that goes far deeper than that. He seems to have isolated himself almost completely from his everyday surroundings as if he's lost all outside contact and exists in a world all his own. All we can do is try to interest him in what's going on around him. It may be a long process but given time, I think he'll snap out of it. In the meantime, try not to make a big issue of his actions and, as I said earlier, bring him back in a couple of weeks.'

As she and Stephen walked back to the car, Alice realised she was becoming more and more discouraged. She had hoped for more from the doctor and what little he had told her went no way towards easing her mind. The feeling of impending disaster was becoming stronger all the time. Something was going to happen, yet she could not imagine what it was, nor when it would come.

★   ★   ★

Over the next few days Alice busied herself in the large gardens while keeping an eye on Stephen. By now, it was clear that he was becoming more and more withdrawn. He would spend hours wandering aimlessly from one room to the next, or standing motionless in front of a large mirror in the hallway, gazing at his reflection. He seldom spoke, even when she asked him directly how he was feeling. At night, she would lie awake for hours, listening intently for any hint of movement outside her door, before sleep finally claimed her.

As far as she could tell, there had been no repeat of what had happened that first night. Whether Stephen slept, or lay awake all night, she had no way of telling, although from his increasingly haggard appearance each morning she gathered he slept little, if at all.

By the middle of the second week in

the Grange, she had made up her mind. The next day she would leave early and drive to London where she would insist he was thoroughly examined by one of the specialists who had treated him after his accident. It was quite clear that the concussion had done far more internal damage to the brain than they had discovered and it was essential he should receive proper treatment.

That evening, she broached the subject with Stephen as they sat before the blazing fire. He listened abstractly as if his thoughts were on other things.

Then, in a tone which seemed oddly calm, he said: 'I don't think that will be necessary. There's nothing they can do for me.'

'Nonsense, of course they can help you,' Alice retorted. 'And once you realise that, you can get on with your life and regain an interest in things. I'm quite sure you'll improve.'

Stephen uttered a faint sigh. 'If you wish me to attend hospital again, very well.' He settled back in his chair, staring into the fire. Knowing that he had no wish to pursue the matter any further, Alice tried to concentrate on reading the book she had taken from the shelf, but it was impossible. Glancing covertly at Stephen, she noticed that his head was cocked a little on one side and was on the point of asking him whether he was still hearing the voices, but wisely decided to remain silent.

The wind had got up and was moaning eerily around the ancient eaves and perhaps that was what he was hearing. Certainly with a little imagination, one could believe there were voices murmuring shrilly around the house. She shook herself mentally. When the clock above the fireplace chimed ten, she got up and went to make their nightly cup of cocoa, which had been a ritual for more years than she could remember.

Handing the mug to Stephen, she noticed that he had drawn his chair closer to the fire and he held the mug in both hands as though warming himself.

'Are you feeling cold, Stephen?' she asked anxiously.

His only reply was a slight nod and for

the first time she noticed how pale his features were; in the ruddy glow of the fire, the deep hollows in his cheeks were even more pronounced than before. On an impulse, she placed her hand on his brow.

'Drink your cocoa and then get to bed,' she said earnestly. 'You seem to have a chill. Once you get a good night's sleep, you'll feel a lot better in the morning.'

She tried to tell herself that this was all that it was — that in spite of all her hopes, the country air was not proving beneficial to him. But why this sensation of apprehension and dread? It was almost as if whatever was troubling Stephen was somehow communicating itself to her.

Once her brother had gone upstairs to his room, she sat for a while in front of the slowly dying fire. The tension and feeling of impending disaster were beginning to grow in her mind. She had the unshakeable conviction that some crisis was about to occur but how she knew it so positively, she couldn't tell.

A glowing ember fell onto the hearth, causing her to jump nervously. The house seemed to be filled with unexplainable noises. On the broad mantelpiece, the ticking of the clock was like a heart beating monotonously against the background of eerie sounds.

Finally, she got up and went around the house, checking that all the doors and windows were secure, then went up to her room, feeling physically and emotionally drained. Yet in spite of the physical weariness, her senses were oddly sharp and alert.

Once undressed, she debated whether to take a couple of sleeping tablets; then decided against it. Lying in that large bed, she tried to focus her thoughts on sleep. Whether this house had anything to do with Stephen's condition, or whether it was an outcome of his accident, she couldn't be sure. But tomorrow she would speak with the specialists and demand some answers. If it was this house, and there was some malign influence at work, then they would have to leave. It would mean another upheaval in their lives, but Stephen's health was paramount.

After a time, she fell into an uneasy doze and when she woke it was still night outside. The white moonlight threw a pattern of dark shadows across the bedroom floor.

She lay quite still, tensed and rigid, struggling to determine what had awakened her. Some time earlier, the wind must have dropped again and only a deep silence reigned within the house. Everything seemed normal. Yet something had intruded into her sleeping mind and had woken her.

Unable to content herself, she slid her legs out of the bed and stood up. For a long moment, she remained by the window, listening, scarcely daring to breathe, unable to move.

Then, pulling herself together, she drew on her robe, crossed to the door, and glanced out. There was no one on the stairs but after a moment she fancied she heard a faint sound from somewhere below. Only one explanation offered itself to her bemused mind. Stephen was awake and moving around as on that previous occasion.

Trying not to make a sound, she descended the stairs, halting at the bottom to look about her. Brilliant moonlight pierced the room with blazing shafts of white, illuminating the interior and making it almost as bright as day. Only the long hallway leading to the front door lay in deep shadow. For an instant, she saw nothing. Then, as her eyes grew accustomed to the brightness, she made out the faint shadow standing in the dimness in front of the mirror.

She opened her mouth to call Stephen's name, then closed it again. There was no point in alarming him in his present condition. Her bare feet made no sound as she padded forward.

Stephen stood absolutely still, his face in shadow, clearly oblivious of her presence. Then something very strange happened. There is a point where normal faith and reason are stretched to their limits and what happens next can never be explained in any rational or logical manner.

At first, Alice thought it was a trick of the moonlight and shadow, for it seemed that Stephen's outline was shimmering oddly, just as she had seen it before when she had stared at his reflection in the mirror. But now it was more definite, more pronounced. He became more and more transparent — until he was gone altogether and the shadowed hallway stood empty.

Standing there, with the cold and chill numbing her limbs, Alice suddenly understood it all and the realisation brought a cold, clammy sweat out of every pore as she tried to choke back the scream that rose in her throat.

Stephen was the one this house had been waiting for with such a terrible expectancy.

A place waiting to be haunted!

Those were the words she had heard on a number of occasions since arriving in the village.

Her brother had not survived that horrific accident. That unidentified body they had found in the mangled, fire-blackened wreck of the car had been no stranger, no acquaintance of his, no hitchhiker he had picked up somewhere along the road.

What unearthly force had produced this manifestation of a living, breathing body for all these months, she did not know. And those voices he had heard, telling him he did not belong here. Their awful meaning was now perfectly clear in her mind.

It was on this earth, among the living, that he did not belong. Now he was truly gone. As she turned and walked slowly back up the stairs, Alice could feel his presence everywhere.

After so many years of waiting, Mexton Grange was now assuredly haunted!

THE ENDING OF
THE TALE

It was late one January evening when
Philip Bransom came across a bookshop
he had not previously visited. It stood in
a little alley well away from the main
London thoroughfares and the dimly-lit
window did nothing to attract any
attention. Indeed, through the dust-
smeared glass, he could make out very
little beyond the fact that almost all the
volumes on display were old and tattered
as if they had been rescued from some
private collection where they had been
left to moulder over many decades.

Perhaps it was this general air of
antiquity and decrepitude that prompted
him to go inside and browse around.
Certainly none of the larger bookstores in
the city had been of any help to him,
containing only the works of modern
authors, and his queries regarding the

novels and short stories of Victor Forrest had been met with blank stares and shakes of the head.

It was dark and dingy inside yet, curiously, it seemed far more spacious than he had expected, viewing it from the alley. There were a few late-night customers browsing among the bookshelves, all muffled up against the winter chill, as he made his way to the rear of the shop where the dusty appearance of the volumes was indicative both of their age and infrequent sale. Fortunately, the majority of the shelves were marked with the relevant subject matter, most dealing with non-fiction works on geography, astronomy and history dating from the eighteenth and nineteenth centuries. Only a small section contained fiction but it was with a strange sense of precognitive excitement that he approached the shelves and bent to examine the titles in the poor light.

Here, as he had expected, he found works by Dickens, Trollope and Wells, together with many authors he had never heard of, and some of the volumes looked so old he felt sure they must be rare arcane first editions. He scanned the titles meticulously, giving a faint sigh of exasperation as he realised their arrangement was completely haphazard and not in alphabetical order of authors as he had hoped.

'Is there something special you are looking for, Mr. Bransom?'

Bransom jumped nervously. He had not heard the shopkeeper approach and, not only had he taken him by surprise, he had called him by name. Despite the abrupt shock of being known by a complete stranger, Bransom managed to keep his composure. Somehow, he kept his voice normal as he asked: 'How do you know my name?'

'I recognised you the minute you stepped into the shop. Retired, a wealthy industrial magnate, collector of rare and obscure works by the lesser-known Victorian masters of ghost and horror stories. If I remember rightly, your particular interest is in the works of Victor Forrest.'

The old man squinted up at Bransom,

eyeing him with a speculative stare.

Seeing no reason to deny this was so, Bransom nodded. By now his eyes had become more accustomed to the gloom inside the shop and he saw that the owner was a small wizened individual of indeterminate age, although his stooped frame and wrinkled features indicated that he could be well over ninety years old.

'Then if you know so much about me,' he said harshly, 'you may be able to help me. There are still some volumes of Forrest's I've been unable to trace and — '

The old man held up a skinny claw. 'I believe I may have just the thing you're looking for. If you come this way, I'll show you.'

Wonderingly, Bransom followed the bent figure through the shop and into a dark corner where a dusty bead curtain secured a narrow doorway. The shopkeeper opened the door and stood on one side, gesturing him to go first.

Like the rest of the shop, the small room was dimly illuminated and Bransom felt a sudden stab of apprehension as he heard the door close softly behind him. Just what was going on? Was this man really a kindred spirit or had he some ulterior motive in bringing him here into what was clearly his inner sanctum?

'Please take a seat, Mr. Bransom.' The shopkeeper pointed towards a rickety chair at the small table.

Before doing so, Bransom threw a swift glance around the room. The first thought which sprang to his mind was that, since this man knew who he was, and that he probably carried a large sum of money on his person, he had an accomplice somewhere nearby, ready to take his well-filled wallet and dump him, unconscious, in some rubbish-filled alley at the rear. But although the room was cluttered with books and papers, many in untidy heaps on the floor and stacked against the walls, he could see no place where anyone might be concealed and, after a momentary pause, he pulled the chair from the table and sat down, still alert for any sign of trouble.

In the yellow light from the paraffin lamp on the table, he studied the old man carefully. The pronounced stoop and wrinkled features betokened great age but the shock of pure white hair and a broad forehead gave him the air of a man possessing a high degree of erudition.

Glancing down, Bransom noticed there was an ashtray beside the lamp containing several cigarette stubs, and he took a cigarette from his gold case and lit it to calm his rising sense of excitement and curiosity. Whether this man had anything of interest to him was a matter of conjecture but it would do no harm to examine anything he had. If there was anything here he required for his collection he might certainly have to pay through the nose for it now that the shopkeeper had recognised him. But he was prepared for that.

'I believe that, like myself, you are an ardent admirer of Victor Forrest,' the old man grunted without looking round. He was searching diligently through a pile of volumes balanced precariously one on top of the other in one corner.

'I first read one of his collections of ghost stories when I was only fourteen,'

Bransom told him, blowing a cloud of blue smoke towards the low ceiling. 'They were utterly fascinating. Since then, I've spent most of my free time collecting as many of his books as I could find, hoping to build up a complete collection. I've even toyed with the idea of writing a biography of him but unfortunately it's proved devilishly difficult to get any real facts about his life, particular the last fifteen years or so. I know he was still writing, but he seemed to have disappeared off the face of the earth.'

'A strange man by all accounts,' the shopkeeper agreed, straightening up. He held a slim volume in his hand.

'He was a genius. To my mind, a far better writer of ghost and horror stories than any of his contemporaries such as Poe and James. Oddly, he never received the recognition that was due to him. Even today, his work is very rarely read. Whether there is any truth in the story that almost all of his stories were based upon real-life events that happened to him, I wouldn't know. But if there is, I can only conclude that, like Poe, the man must have spent the best part of his life on the brink of insanity.'

'I feel this will be of interest to you.' The old man pushed the book towards him across a table. 'It's extremely rare. In fact, I doubt if you could find another copy anywhere outside of the British Museum.'

Blowing the accumulation of fine dust from the cover, Bransom held it close to the lamp and glanced at the title, uttering a low whistle of surprise and amazement. 'This must be the last collection of ghost stories Forrest wrote,' he muttered incredulously. 'I've heard of it, naturally. But I thought it had never been published. From what I've read, he was working on it at the time of his death in eighteen ninety-seven.' He turned the pages almost reverently.

'You're quite right. There was to be twenty short stories in that volume but as you can see, there are only nineteen. The final one was apparently begun, but never finished.'

Despite a sense of revulsion at the other's appearance, Bransom felt a sudden surge of excitement at the man's revelation. 'Can you tell me anything at all about Forrest?'

The old man's glance flicked to the ancient, ornate clock on the wall which, in spite of its obvious age, still seemed to be keeping remarkably accurate time. His manner implied that it was almost closing time. Nevertheless, he gave a brief nod.

'I'll tell you all I know, Mr. Bransom.' Bransom found himself staring into the old man's eyes and, no matter how hard he tried, it was impossible to tear his gaze from that mesmeric stare. He seemed to hear the wheezing voice speaking to him from a vast, echoing distance.

'As you may know, Forrest was born in Cornwall, near the coast, spent most of his life there, gathering many of the old Cornish tales which he then transcribed under his own name. He never married, preferring life as a recluse, although we do know that he sometimes journeyed to London where he met several of his fellow writers such as Dickens and the young Bram Stoker. Then, for some reason, he left Cornwall and took up residence in Bramlington Hall, somewhere in Essex, and it was there he wrote his best work.'

The old man paused, his gaze still fixed hypnotically on Bransom. Leaning forward, he tapped the volume in front of him. 'If you read these, you'll find that he uses that house, very thinly disguised, in nearly all of the stories. Indeed, there are some of the local folk around there who claim that his ghost still haunts that place but I wouldn't put too much credence in such wild tales. Certainly I know that Bramlington Hall has never been occupied since the day he died there. By all accounts, it has been left to rot and decay and nothing in it has been touched for a century. It's exactly as he left it.'

Bransom felt his interest quickened. He had already known something of what the old shopkeeper had told him, but he had not been aware of the fact that everything in Bramlington Hall had been left exactly as it was when Victor Forrest had died. It was immediately apparent to him that if the manuscript of Forrest's last unfinished story still existed, that was where it would be and, as far as he was concerned, it was a prize worth having.

He grew aware that the old man was

thrusting the slim volume towards him, saying throatily: 'Take this, Mr. Bransom, from one admirer of Victor Forrest to another. I'm sure it will prove of more value to you than to an old man such as myself.'

'But I can't take it for nothing,' Bransom protested. 'At least, let me give you something for it. The book must be priceless to any collector.'

Almost before he was aware of it, Bransom clasped the book in both hands and the next moment, totally unaware of any transition, he found himself on the narrow lane, staring about him in shock and bewilderment. He had no knowledge of how he got there. There was no memory in his mind of having passed through that doorway, between the shelves in the shop, and out in the open. He stood there for several moments, swaying slightly as he fought to regain his mental balance.

Drawing in a deep breath of the chill night air, he turned slowly to look behind him and it was then that a shock of horror replaced the amazement, for where he had thought the bookshop to be was an abandoned building with boarded-up windows and a splintered wooden door sagging from rusted hinges. His mind in turmoil, he slowly paced the entire length of the lane, now unsure of his own sanity, for all the tumbledown buildings had clearly been empty for decades.

Had he dreamed it all, or had it been an hallucination? No; that wasn't the explanation for he still clutched the precious volume in his hands. Unless he had, somehow, suffered a temporary lapse of memory inside the shop and after leaving, he had walked some distance without realising it, only coming to his senses in this alley which, although it closely resembled that in which the bookshop was located, was actually some distance away.

Struggling to orientate himself, he noticed an old man eyeing him curiously from a few feet away. Approaching him, Bransom asked casually: 'Could you by any chance tell me if there was ever a bookshop in this street?' In spite of his efforts, his voice sounded totally unlike his own.

'A bookshop?' For a moment, the passer-by looked surprised. Then, as if some recollection had suddenly come to him, he gave a terse nod. 'Why yes, there used to be one right there.' He pointed to the boarded-up building a few yards away. 'But it closed down nigh on eighty years ago, back in the early twenties. That must've been before you were born, mister. Why do you ask?'

'It was nothing, really,' Bransom mumbled. 'I've heard my father speak of it and just wondered if it was still in existence.'

Totally confused and more than a little frightened, Bransom muttered his thanks and hurried away. All the way back to his apartment, he strove to rationalise what had happened. The possession of the volume was concrete proof that he had neither dreamed, nor imagined, everything. Someone had clearly wanted him to have this book, but from what obscure motive he could not imagine. Gradually, however, his initial feeling of fear and mystification gave way to one of intense elation.

Furthermore, he had learned certain

vital details about Victor Forrest, which he had not previously known. Bramlington Hall. The name popped unbidden into his mind. If it was indeed true that it was there Forrest had spent the later years of his life, hidden away from society, and dying before he could complete that final manuscript, and if that house was still standing, *and nothing had been touched or removed since Forrest's death a century earlier*, it might just be possible that the original manuscript, in Forrest's own handwriting, was still there.

When he retired that night, he felt like a man on the brink of some amazing discovery. Priceless as the book he now had was, that original manuscript was even more so. Not that he would ever sell it. Money now meant little to him except as a means of getting anything he wanted.

Almost asleep, he wondered how he could discover where Bramlington Hall was. Somewhere in Essex that old man said. In the morning, he would consult a map and then, perhaps, drive out to take a look around. With the means he had, it should be possible to buy the place and live there himself. It should be comparatively easy to ensure that the purchase price included all the contents and if he should come across any of Forrest's original manuscripts, they would then belong to him.

He fell asleep, and dreamed he was walking through wild countryside, along narrow, winding paths, through patches of woodland and across rolling fields — and there was a solitary figure some distance ahead. In his dream, it seemed essential that he should catch up with the moving shape for there was something of great importance he had to ask him. But no matter how fast he tried to go, the figure still remained as far away as ever. Then, breasting a low hill, he saw that the dark shape disappeared but there, below him, standing in the extensive grounds, stood an ancient, turreted house.

He had no doubt that this was the place he was looking for, Bramlington Hall, though he couldn't tell how he was so certain. The great door stood open, a rectangular mass of shadow, beckoning him forward with a compulsion he was unable to resist, even though an inner voice warned him that something dreadful lurked within. Stepping inside, into a great room whose gloomy corners seemed to conceal all manner of things, he thought he heard a voice whose timbre dismayed him, saying: 'Welcome to Bramlington Hall, Philip Bransom. Now that you are finally come, my tale may indeed be ended.'

The dark figure he had vainly pursued across the desolate moorland emerged from the shadows carrying something awful in its hands as it advanced towards him. Just in time, his sharp inarticulate cry brought him shudderingly awake.

If the dream were some kind of premonition, it confirmed that he needed information concerning Bramlington Hall. He lay for a while until his thudding heart-beat had slowed to normal, then glanced at the clock on his bedside table. It was only a little after three and still dark out-side. Turning over, he fell into an uneasy doze. Again he dreamed, but this time it commenced almost where the earlier night-mare had ended. He was standing inside that huge room. There was a fire blazing in the wide hearth and the flickering gas-lights around the walls threw weird, dancing shadows into every corner. Fearfully, he looked about him, expecting to see that ghastly figure moving towards him. But the room was empty.

Again, some powerful coercion impelled him towards a door on the far side, a door that stood ajar. It opened as he approached, swinging back noiselessly of its own voli-tion. Beyond, a long corridor, lined with sombre portraits, lay in almost total dark-ness, the only illumination coming from a single wall lamp at the far end where a second door stood open. In his dream, his unwilling feet carried him along the corridor and through the door into a smaller room, just as poorly lit as the first.

A man sat at the long table, his back to Bransom, his head bent forward a little, seemingly oblivious to Bransom's pres-ence. Going forward, he caught a glimpse of the man's features, and recognised them at once from a faded picture he had seen in *The Illustrated London News* as those of Victor Forrest. The writer was scribbling furiously, pausing only to dip his quill in the large bottle of ink beside his right elbow.

Drawing nearer, Bransom stared over Forrest's shoulder at the manuscript, watching him with an awe-struck fascination as the words flowed from beneath the point of the quill. Then, slowly, Forrest turned his head and, in the instant between sleeping and jerking awake, Bransom saw that it was the face of a dead man which leered up at him, and the voice which issued from the bloodless lips, deep and sepulchral said: 'Now, after all these long years, comes the ending of the tale.'

This time when he woke, he remained awake, with the covers pulled up to his chin, until the cheerless grey light of dawn seeped through the windows. He felt shaken, yet just as determined as ever to locate Forrest's last residence and, if possible, buy it. After a hasty breakfast, he went to one of the many libraries in the middle of the city where he consulted some of the original early editions of 1897 newspapers, searching for any record of Forrest's obituary.

It was almost half an hour later when he eventually came across it, tucked away on one of the inside pages. There was only a single, brief paragraph stating that Victor Meltham Forrest had died on February second, 1897 at Bramlington Hall in the county of Essex at the age of seventy-seven. There was only a short description of his literary output, but accompanying the write-up was a faded photograph of Bramlington Hall.

Staring down at it, Bransom felt a little shiver of ice brush along his spine for he immediately recognised it as that which he had seen in his dream. Identical in every detail, the picture bore the caption: '*Bramlington Hall, six miles east of Frampton in Essex, where Victor Forrest spent his final years.*'

Glancing surreptitiously around him to ensure that he could not be observed, Bransom quietly tore the picture from the page and thrust it into his pocket before leaving hurriedly. At last, he had the clue he needed. What worried him, however, was how he could possibly have dreamed of this place, a place he had never seen before, one about whose existence he had not even known until the previous day. Was it possible to dream of the future — and in such minute, actual detail?

It was a question to which there was no answer and, with an effort, he put it out of his mind. Whatever was happening to him, however weird and strange it may seem, he had to go along with it. Returning home, he took a large-scale map of Essex and the surrounding counties from the shelf and leafed through it rapidly. There was no mention of Frampton in the index but after perusing each of the grid squares carefully, he suddenly came upon it, so close to the edge of the map that it was extremely difficult to make it out.

Now he had his location and nothing would satisfy him but to drive out that very day and set things in motion.

★   ★   ★

Bransom recognised the house the moment he saw it standing stark and forbidding in the pale winter sunlight. It looked even more ominous and uncanny than in the

71

fading photograph. Tall, sombre gables rose on either side of the massive oaken front door; small, leaded windows, half-hidden by the clinging ivy, stared like sightless eyes across the sloping, overgrown lawn; high chimneys like pointing, accusing fingers, thrust skyward from the roof.

Stepping out of the car to stand beside the estate agent he had found in Frampton, he felt a surge of excitement and achievement at having finally tracked it down. It was undoubtedly in urgent need of major repairs. More than a score of the slates were missing from that part of the roof you could see and there were doubtless many more on the other side. Two of the high windows were merely gaping holes where the glass had fallen from the rotten wood; and as to the state of the interior, he couldn't guess.

Following the direction of his gaze, William Norton said, almost apologetically: 'You have to understand, Mr. Bransom, that since Victor Forrest's death a century ago, this property has lain untenanted and untouched. To be quite honest, I'm surprised anyone is still interested in it. It has some potential, I'll admit, but as you can see for yourself, it will require a considerable sum to restore it to anything like its former condition.'

Bransom gave a negligent shrug to indicate that money was no object. 'The building itself is of only secondary importance to me,' he replied. 'My main purpose in wishing to purchase it is that it was here that Victor Forrest wrote his best work. You know something about him, I presume?' He stared directly at Norton as he spoke.

'Why, yes. A writer of Victorian horror stories, wasn't he? I can't say I'm all that keen on his stories. A little too bloodthirsty for my liking, I'm afraid.'

'Well, I suppose that's all a matter of taste,' Bransom declared.

'Perhaps you'd like to go inside and take a look around,' Norton suggested.

'Certainly.' Bransom nodded but made no move to follow the estate agent. He turned very slowly to scrutinise his surroundings and the lie of the countryside. They had driven out to the house along a narrow winding road with tall hedgerows on either side so that he had not been able to view much but here, where they were more in the open, he noticed the dark mass of a wood crowning a low hill to the south and the sight of it stirred strange emotions within him. It was almost exactly as he had seen it in his dream. Had he been asked at that moment, he believed he could have actually described the contours of the land that lay out of sight beyond the hill.

Standing a few feet away, Norton eyed him with a renewed interest. Bramlington Hall had been on the books of Henson and Norton since his grandfather's time and there had never been any enquiries made about it that he could recall. Old Mr. Henson had sometimes spoken of it before he had retired some thirty years earlier, how at first they had thought it would be snapped up fairly quickly considering that Forrest was something of a celebrity in his day. But nothing had ever materialised and the deeds had lain, gathering dust at the bottom of the drawer in the office filing cabinet.

If he could palm it off on to this client,

it would certainly be a feather in his cap. Bransom looked like a man who had plenty of ready cash and who, for some reason known only to himself, seemed to have set his heart on buying the dilapidated old place.

'You seem to have gone to extraordinary lengths to locate Bramlington Hall,' he said finally as Bransom, who had been staring down at the old picture, refolded the piece of paper and slipped it into his pocket. 'You aren't, by chance, related to Forrest in any way?'

'Not at all.' Bransom fell into step beside him. 'I've been intensely interested in him and his stories for most of my life. He turned out a prolific amount of novels and short stories you know, many of them under various pseudonyms, but instantly recognisable to anyone conversant with his style. Over the years I've made quite a collection so I guess you could call me an authority on the man. From what I've learned, he spent the last fifteen years of his life here. Now you can possibly understand why I insisted that all of the contents be included in the purchase price.'

Norton fumbled in his pocket for the keys. 'I'm quite sure there will be no problems about that. Enquiries were made at the time of his death, but no relatives could be traced and no one has come forward since then to lay any claim to his estate.'

He unlocked the heavy door and stood on one side for Bransom to proceed. Inside, it was quite dark for a number of the windows were tightly shuttered and those that were not, were very small, letting in little of the sunlight. Norton deliberately left the front door open so that more of the light entered. One glance was sufficient for Bransom to recognise the room although the state of neglect and decay into which it had fallen over the decades, gave it a somewhat different aspect to that which he had seen in his dreams. Dust and cobwebs were everywhere, festooning the antique Victorian furniture, clogging the corners with sticky strands. Mildewed wallpaper hung in long strips from the walls and there was a mound of grey ash in the wide stone hearth.

Here, in places, the carpet had rotted away; in others, the once-rich colours had faded almost completely. Damp and weather had attacked the window frames and much of the lead beading had come away from the outer supports, leaving the glass in danger of falling out with the next gale. Wrinkling his nose, Bransom moved towards the far door. All around him, the room with its stale unmoving air and memories of its long-dead owner, still seemed horribly alive. Even though Victor Forrest had been dead for a century, Bransom had the feeling that some part of him was still around, watching him.

Throwing open the door, he stared along the strangely familiar corridor. One or two portraits still hung on the walls, but most of them had fallen from their hangings where these had given way, breaking loose from the crumbling plaster. The door at the far end was locked but Norton produced the key and inserted it into the lock. It turned protestingly, grating loudly in the silence.

'I understand this was Forrest's study,' the estate agent said as they went inside.

'It was here he was reputedly found, slumped over the table, evidently having died while still writing. I'm not certain as to the cause of death, but it must have been sudden and entirely unexpected.'

Bransom looked around the room, taking in every detail. He expressed a further faint shock of surprise. The room, although long closed and showing similar signs of decay as the other, with ugly damp stains on the walls and a sagging ceiling, still bore signs of use. There were papers still on the table; a quill pen near them and a large inkbottle, its contents long since dried out to papery residue. An open book lay beside the papers and there were several others, all closed, arranged in a neat pile. A layer of dust covered every-thing, including the paraffin lamp in the middle, its glass cover fly-specked and almost opaque with the accumulated grime of several years of contamination.

'This is the room where he was working when he died,' Bransom said, feeling a little tingle run along his nerves as his voice was thrown back mockingly from the walls.

'It would appear so,' nodded Norton, who advanced to the table and was examining the various papers lying there. He coughed as the white dust caught at the back of his throat. 'As you can see, this page ends in mid-sentence and the last word is almost obliterated by a blob of ink.' He held out the sheet towards Bransom.

The paper was yellow with age and the ink on it faded somewhat over the years. But there was plenty of evidence to show that Forrest must have been writing it when death had overtaken him so abruptly. There was a definite increase in illegibility towards the end, until the final sentence was almost unrecognisable, the writing having degenerated into an untidy scrawl and where the final word was there was simply an irregular inkblot, ending in a line which extended almost the full width of the page.

Replacing it on the table with the others, he said: 'How long will it be before I can move in?'

'You've already made up your mind to take this place, then?'

'Certainly.'

'Then I think I can have all the papers ready for your signature by the end of the week.' Norton glanced meaningfully around the room before adding, 'As you've seen, there are a lot of repairs necessary before this house is really habitable. There's no electricity laid on, I'm afraid. I'd like to be able to suggest local builders to do the work but I'm afraid you won't get anyone from Frampton or thereabouts to come here.'

'Why on earth not?' Bransom asked, surprised. 'I'd be prepared to pay well for any work which has to be undertaken.'

Norton shook his head decisively. 'Money isn't the problem, Mr. Bransom. This house has a bad reputation in these parts, has had ever since the last owner died. I don't believe in any of these weird tales myself, you understand. But the folk here are a superstitious lot and things have been seen and heard which, if true, defy all explanation.'

Accompanying him to the front door, Bransom asked: 'What sort of things?'

The estate agent seemed to be trying

not to frown and Bransom stared at him intently as he went on: 'You'd think the people around here would have been honoured to have had a Victorian literary man living here but my guess is that they didn't take to some of the things he wrote about, especially when it was quite obvious he incorporated this house and countryside in many of his stories, even claimed they were mostly based on fact. Perhaps it was that which gave rise to the kind of tales that have been spread over the years. A lot of folk, some well educated people, reckon they have seen him walking the moors and in that wood on the Hill. Others claim to have seen lights in these windows at dead of night.'

'So they believe he still haunts the Hall?'

Norton shrugged. 'It would seem so. Not that you'll get any of them to talk about it, particularly to an outsider.'

Following the estate agent to the waiting car, Bransom decided that, once the Hall had been repaired to his satisfaction and he was settled in, he would have a talk with some of the locals as it was possible he might be able to glean some information from them concerning the long-dead author. Even if this was only in the form of whispered spectral tales, they might contain some snippets of fact that could be of interest.

It was a full month before Bransom finally moved into Bramlington Hall. The estate agent had proved right in his statement that he would obtain no help from any builders in the vicinity and he had been forced to engage men from London. The restoration had been a stupendous task, yet he had allowed no expense to deter him, pushing the workmen as hard as he could, growing more and more irritated at any delays due to the inclement weather. Towards the final stages of the work, he moved into a hotel in Frampton, determined to keep a close eye on the place, to ensure that nothing that had belonged to Victor Forrest was touched.

It was while he was there that he began to pick up some of the old rumours, which Norton had briefly mentioned when they had first met. A few of the stories were clearly nothing more than hackneyed country lore such as persisted in many parts of rural England where very old houses were the topic of conversation. He tried to dismiss tales of the dark figure witnessed by late-night travellers on the narrow country road which passed across the Moors, but found this difficult to do since they brought back vivid memories of that hideous dream and the strange manner by which he had obtained the last book of stories Victor Forrest had written.

Despite what Norton had told him, a small number of the villagers seemed willing to talk to him, especially after he had bought them a few drinks in the small, picturesque hotel bar with its massive oak beams and blazing fire. One old local was particularly voluble when it came to describing certain odd things that had happened over the years.

'You city folk may laugh at some o' the things we believe in, Mister,' he said in a low, throaty whisper. They were seated at one of the tables on the night before Bransom was due to move into Bramlington Hall. 'But out here we are a lot closer to nature and we don't mock the idea that unquiet spirits often return, specially if there were somethin' on earth they left undone at the time o' their deaths.'

'You've seen this ghost yourself?' Bransom asked, placing another drink in front of his companion.

'Aye, I've seen him. More'n once. Sometimes in that wood yonder, other times driftin' across the moors. Whatever it is he's come back for, it ain't finished yet. If it were, he'd now rest peaceful with the others in the churchyard.'

'But what makes you so sure it's him?' Bransom enquired. 'It could have been anyone you saw, walking on the moors.' He had dismissed the idea that all of this was nothing more than imagination. Apparently, it had happened too many times over the years for everyone who claimed to have seen the figure to have suffered some kind of hallucination. But he was still unwilling to accept that it was Forrest's ghost that they had all seen. But if it were, that would really be an experience.

'It were him all right.' The old man

gave a toothless grin as he drank down half of his drink in a couple of swallows. 'Who else could it be all these years? And if you really want proof, ask Ted yonder.' He jerked a thumb towards the barman. 'He don't like talkin' about it, but seein' as you will be livin' there, he might tell you what he saw last Eastertide.'

Bransom threw a quick glance in the barman's direction. He had already spoken with him on several occasions since arriving at the hotel: a short, bespectacled man in his early forties, yet his thick, pure-white hair added a couple of decades to his age. Bransom had found him to be talkative enough when discussing mundane topics and willing enough to point out places of interest around Frampton. But not once had he spoken of Bramlington Hall and its long-dead owner.

At the moment, there were no other customers at the bar and, pushing back his chair, Bransom walked over, taking his half-empty glass with him.

'Yes, sir.' Moving over to where he stood, the barman gave him a curiously penetrating stare, obviously having heard the topic of conversation between Bransom and the old man still seated at the table.

'I've been told you had a strange experience last Easter,' Bransom said without preamble. 'I wonder if you'd care to tell me about it.'

The barman hesitated, nervously wiping the top of the counter with a blue cloth. Then he said harshly: 'If you have been listening to some of the tales old Walter's been on about, I'd forget them if I were you, sir. He's not quite right in the head and he'll spin any old yarn to anyone foolish enough to listen.'

'Perhaps he would,' Bransom replied. 'But from what I've heard, there have been far too many sightings for them all to be put down to imagination.'

A serious expression flitted across the barman's ruddy features. He stood quite still for several seconds, his fingers twitching nervously where they held the bar cloth. Then he gave a brief nod, with a sidelong glance along the bar. 'There isn't much to tell, and I'm only telling you now because you're hell-bent on living in that accursed place. Believe me, if there was anything I could say to dissuade you, I would.'

Bransom finished his drink and pushed the empty glass across the counter, waiting for the refill before saying: 'Was it something you saw in the Hall?'

'Aye, it were.' The other's voice was little more than a whisper as if he were afraid of being overheard by other customers in the bar. Giving Bransom his change, he went on: 'It's not something I like to talk about, least of all remember. Maybe you won't believe this, sir, but before that night this hair of mine was jet black. Now it's pure white.' He broke off to serve one of the locals, then came back, his face etched with deep planes of shadow as he rested his elbows on the bar and leaned forward, thrusting his face close to Bransom's.

'Like Walter says, it were Eastertide and there was a full moon that night. I'd been over to Westford that day to arrange for several more barrels to be delivered before the weekend and was driving back along the road past the Hall when I spotted a light in the windows downstairs.

I knew, of course, that the place was empty, had been since before I was born, so it struck me as highly strange that there should be anyone there. We'd heard nothing of anyone buying the place and moving in, so I stopped the car and went to take a look. I reckoned it could be no one from Frampton hereabouts; nobody'll go near that place, especially after dark. The moon was pretty well up by that time so there was plenty of light to see by and even before I got to the window, I knew I hadn't been mistaken. I'd thought it must have just been the moonlight reflected off the glass if the light was coming from inside the room and it wasn't the yellow light you'd expect from candles or a lamp, it was a red light.'

The barman's voice dropped even lower as he went on so that Bransom had to strain to catch the words. 'The light was quite plain, a flickering sort of glow and the only thing I could think of was that the place was on fire. Anyway, I got up to the window and risked a quick look inside. There was a fire in that room alright but it was burning in the grate and

I swear to God that everything there was just as it must've been nearly a hundred years ago! All gleaming and new. There was a man sitting in the chair at the table, his back to the window, but even though I couldn't see his face I knew who he was. Victor Forrest come back to haunt the Hall. I am no believer in ghosts and the like, take my word for that, and I swear I'd never touched a drop all that day. Don't ask me how long I stood there, shaking like a leaf. It seemed like hours, but it couldn't have been. I knew I had to be seeing things, but then he turned and looked straight at me as if he knew I was there and his face — '

He broke off sharply, hesitated for a moment, then poured himself a whiskey from the bottle behind the bar, downing it in a single gulp, grimacing as the raw liquor hit the back of his throat. There was a faint sheen of sweat on his forehead.

'Go on,' Bransom prompted when the other made no move to speak. 'What more did you see?'

The barman swallowed twice before speaking in a hoarse whisper. 'It were the face of a devil, a madman. Then he stood up and I thought he was coming to the window and, dear God, my feet wouldn't budge. But then he stopped and gave the most horrible laugh I've ever heard. I saw that he was pointing towards the far side of the room and there was . . . there was another figure there — a body hanging from one of the ceiling beams. That was enough to send me running from that terrible place, back into the car. Don't ask me how I managed to drive here because I don't remember a thing. It was the first, and only, time I drank myself stupid. Do you blame me?'

★   ★   ★

The barman's story was still uppermost in Bransom's mind when he moved into Bramlington Hall the next day. The roof had been repaired, all the broken windows replaced and everything inside had been cleaned from top to bottom. The whole of the upper floor had been modernised to his own taste but the large room downstairs and that which had been

Forrest's study had been restored just as they had been in their Victorian splendour with their wainscoted walls and high vaulted ceilings and the original furniture. Bransom viewed them with a sense of pride, which fully compensated for the prodigious amount which had been spent on their restoration.

For a week, his routine proceeded with the utmost equanimity, his time being spent mainly on going through Forrest's papers, concentrating primarily on the numerous letters he had written to his various contemporaries. The closely written pages of the final unfinished story, he had put on one side, saving that until last, intending to read through it when both his mood and the atmosphere within the old house were exactly right. This was something he meant to savour to the full, reading a manuscript which no one else in the world had ever seen.

Each night he slept soundly in the large bedroom to the rear. Nothing happened to disturb him during the night; there were no unexplainable sounds on the stairs or in any of the lower rooms, no ghostly footsteps on the broad landing outside his door. Gradually, as the days passed, he put the barman's story from his mind.

Then, one morning, the first incident occurred which, although apparently trivial at the time, assumed a preternatural significance in relation to later events. It was so slight as to be almost negligible. Coming downstairs, he went into the study where he had spent the previous evening arranging all the books on the well-stocked shelves. It was when he approached the table that he noticed that certain of the closely-written pages were oddly disarranged. He felt certain that he had left them in a neat pile beside the lamp but now a number of them lay scattered on the tabletop.

Had he been walking in his sleep during the night and come down here to read through them, making his own way back to bed and remembering nothing of the event? It seemed the only logical explanation for there were no draughts in the room now which could have disturbed the papers and, as far as he was aware, the night had been completely calm.

Gathering up the sheets, he arranged them in the correct order and placed a heavy glass inkbottle on top. After breakfast, he decided to walk into the village for further supplies. It was a fresh, sunny morning, mild for the time of year, with just a slight breeze blowing from the southwest. Taking the path across the coarse grass, he climbed a low rise to where the wood sprawled across the crown of the hill. There was a narrow trail leading through the trees, winding erratically in and out among the huge, gnarled trunks, which he knew would take him down the further side of the hill into Frampton.

Stepping into the chill shade of the overhanging branches, he immediately became aware of a curious fact. A few moments earlier, there had been the unmistakable sound of a tractor in the distance where some farmer was preparing the ground for early sowing. Now, all sound ceased although he was only a few yards inside the wood. The air had suddenly become very still and cold and he gave a little shiver. Something more than the thickly intertwining boughs shutting out much of the direct sunlight was amiss; something long-dead yet horribly alive was watching him.

He felt extraordinarily severed from all touch of natural intimacy; and yet he was not alone. Something was here; something malevolent, moving up closer to him through the trees.

The faint light from the sun glowed greenly through the overhead canopy of newly budded leaves and, glancing along the path ahead of him, he suddenly saw a man standing there beside an ancient oak. The glimpse he got of the man's face was brief but he saw enough to know that it was undoubtedly Victor Forrest and, for a moment, sheer terror clutched at him as he saw the expression of feral malice on the bearded features. Instinctively, he took a backward step and almost lost balance as his foot stepped on a thick twig, snapping it with a sharp, explosive crack. For a second, his glance turned away from the ghostly shape and when he lifted his head and looked again, there was no one there.

His heart was hammering wildly in his throat and it was a full minute before he managed to regain his composure. Had there really been someone standing there? Or had it been nothing more than a combination of the straggly bushes and out-thrusting low branches which had supplied his imagination with the figure that had been on his mind for several months?

Steeling himself, he walked towards the spot but there was nothing there. Thick grass grew around the bole of the tree and there was no indication that this had been crushed by anyone standing there a few moments before. Yet the image had been so vivid and lifelike that he found it difficult to convince himself it had been nothing more than a trick of the light.

He hurried on into the village where he purchased his requirements from the small grocery store. The man behind the counter eyed him curiously.

'How are you finding things at the Hall, Mr. Bransom?' he asked.

'Everything seems fine now that all the

repairs been carried out,' Bransom replied, taking his change. 'Why do you ask?' The man's tone had implied there was something more to his question than just making polite conversation.

'It's nothing, really. Just that there've been a lot more folk as have seen him lately. Almost as if he knows someone's moved in and he's — ' The storekeeper broke off in mid-sentence, obviously wishing he hadn't asked the question in the first place.

'Go on,' Bransom urged. 'What were you going to say?'

The man hesitated uncertainly, running his fingers over his stubbled chin. 'It's nothing but old legends. You know how these stories grow over the years. Those tales he wrote. I've read a few of them myself. Not the sort of thing you'd read alone at night, if you take my meaning. And they say he didn't really make them up; he was just writing down things had happened to himself.'

'So perhaps he was. I've heard all that before. That's not what you had in mind, is it? There's something else.'

'Aye. But I reckon you'll know more about that than me. Talk is that he were writing something when he died and he can't rest until he's finished it. Around these parts, we believe that an unquiet spirit means mischief. If I were you, I'd be very careful.'

This sounded so much like patronage that Bransom felt a surge of anger as he left the shop. He had fought his way up in life from virtually nothing to become one of the wealthiest men in the country, he had gambled large sums without the blink of an eye, he had been utterly ruthless in getting everything he had set his mind on, even to crushing anyone who stood in his way; and now these country bumpkins with their weird beliefs were trying to tell him that he couldn't take care of himself. If Victor Forrest was really haunting this region because he hadn't completed that final story, then let him come back by all means, and finish it.

Leaving the village, Bransom took the roundabout route back to the Hall, following the road for four miles and then striking out across the moors, keeping the wood on his right. By the time he reached the house, dark storm clouds had appeared on the southeastern horizon and a low rumble of thunder echoed over the distant hills. Hurrying inside as the first large drops of rain began to fall, he lit several of the candles and placed them in the large room where they gave the maximum light. Sometime in the future, he decided, he would have to arrange to have electricity connected to the house. It would detract from the old Victorian charm but the convenience would more than compensate for that.

Lighting a fire in the wide hearth, he waited for the first logs to catch before going into the study where he scooped up the pages containing Forrest's incomplete story, carrying them back to the fire. Sinking into one of the chairs, he drew it closer to the hearth and settled down to read through the manuscript.

The writing, though faded a little with time, was in a bold, clear hand with each letter meticulously formed so that it was still perfectly legible. In the dimness of the room with only the faint crackling of the blazing wood and the intermittent rumble of thunder in the distance to break the silence, Bransom was soon immersed in a tale of horror that surpassed all of the other stories he had read. He had deliberately chosen this particular time to read it since he was peculiarly sensitive to atmosphere and the flickering candles and the occasional lightning flash illuminating the dark wainscoting and long tapestries around the room gave him the certain ambience he needed to gain the maximum effect.

It was a chilling tale entitled *The Midnight Visitor*, written in Forrest's inimitable style, telling of an old, isolated house on the moors and its evil occupant who, even after death had claimed him, continued to haunt the place, waiting with infinite patience to wreak vengeance upon anyone who had wronged him in the past.

Outside, the storm surged nearer, the lightning flashes more vivid and numerous, the thunderclaps more deafening, but Bransom was scarcely aware of it. Around him, the room seemed to have grown darker. He turned his head slowly and peered around. Was it night already, or was it merely the blackness of the storm clouds? He thrust the long brass poker into the logs, sending sparks swirling up the chimney, but the gloom continued to thicken and encroach.

He shook his head and, for some unaccountable reason, began to drift, his head nodding forward onto his chest. One of the logs fell onto the hearth, jerking him upright. Stretching out his leg, he pushed the log away from the edge of the hearth with his foot. The air inside the room had suddenly grown a lot colder. It was an icy chill which struck deep into his bones, and even the fire seemed to have lost much of its heat.

Turning up the wick of the lamp, he sat back to read the final page, gripping the flimsy sheets tightly, feeling his arms and fingers oddly numb.

*   *   *

'Iliff closed his eyes tightly so that he might not see what was in the room with him. *His consternation had concentrated into a single thought in his whirling mind. He had thought the house to be empty; to have lain untenanted for almost a century; the rooms devoid of all occupants, the eaves left to the nocturnal swifts and bats.*

'*Why had he given way to the insane impulse which had caused him to buy this old place? Why had he not listened to those who averred that old Silas Vellner still walked these rooms and corridors, his restless spirit confined to this earthly plane until he had earned his entry into that everlasting hell which undoubtedly awaited him?*

'*With an effort, he forced his eyes open, staring around him and, as he had guessed, the room was empty. The flickering light from the candles showed shadows that had no right to be there. He stood quite still for several seconds until his racing heart had ceased its hammering and his nerves were back to normal.*

'*Controlling himself, he advanced towards the table, shivering a little in the blast of cold air which suddenly swirled around him. It was then, out of the corner of his eye, that he caught a glimpse of —* '

★   ★   ★

Here, the writing ended in an ugly blot where the quill had splintered as Forrest had slumped forward over the table the instant that death had overtaken him.

What more had he hoped to write? Bransom wondered. What other words and phrases had been in his mind, waiting to be transferred from his brain to his fingers and thence onto the paper to complete this tale? There was no way anyone would ever know. Those words were lost and gone forever.

Shivering in the sudden cold, Bransom leaned forward a little, staring into the fire which now seemed to give out no warmth at all in spite of the crackling flames leaping around the blazing logs. The room was now almost completely dark, yet he could still see the candle flames burning as brightly as before — but now they were mere pinpoints of light in the all-pervading gloom. His eyelids drooped and, without being aware of it, he was asleep.

When he woke, an indeterminate time later, it was with the sharp conviction that something was wrong. With an effort, he levered himself upright in the chair. Instinctively, he glanced down at his hands where they rested on his lap. They were empty. Yet he had been reading that manuscript before he had fallen asleep.

Where were the pages?

Getting up, he searched the floor around the chair but there was no sign of them. Had they slipped from his fingers and fallen in the fire? There were no draughts in the room, the air was perfectly still, and it seemed unlikely they had all been consumed to ashes, leaving no trace on the hearth.

Puzzled, he tentatively crossed the room to where the door leading into the hall was open. Surely he closed it behind him when he brought the sheets in from the study. Returning to the table, he picked up the lamp and held it out in front of him as he made his way towards the study. The door at the far end of the passage was half-open and yellow light showed through from the room beyond.

Pushing open the door, he went inside. There was a lamp burning brilliantly on the table although he was certain he had left the room in darkness. Near the lamp were the pages he had read earlier in front of the fire and beside them was a brand-new quill and the inkbottle, now clearly filled with fresh ink!

Bransom sucked in a deep breath to steady himself. What the hell was going on? Either he had brought the manuscript back here while still in some kind of semi-sleeping state during which he remembered nothing, or there was some truth in what the villagers spoke about in hushed whispers and —

A movement caught his eye at the far side of the study where the shadows were deepest. He turned his head quickly as the tall gaunt figure stepped towards him, the oddly familiar face set in a diabolical leer, the deep-set eyes burning with a malevolent triumph. Bransom stood rigidly by the table. There was a ravening turmoil inside his mind but his body felt nothing, utterly numbed by the arctic chill that had suddenly enveloped him. He tried to speak but his lips refused to move; only his eyes seemed capable of movement. The advancing figure bore something in its hands; a long coil of rope, fashioned into a noose.

A little voice in his mind shrieked at him to turn and run, to get out of the house, out into the sanity of the night and away from this terrible place. But he could not move, even when the noose slipped over his head and tightened around his neck. Hands colder than ice and as strong as steel closed around his waist and bore him across the room until he was standing almost directly beneath the thick oaken beam across the ceiling, over which the rope had been thrown.

A long second that seemed to stretch itself out into an eternity passed and then the noose tightened abruptly, crushing his windpipe as he was drawn upward until his thrashing legs dangled inches from the floor. It did not take long for him to die, for the darkness to swallow him up completely.

Below the gently swaying body, a single sheet of paper lay on the table in front of the empty chair. On it, written in a bold and well-formed hand, the ink still gleaming wetly in the lamplight, was the ending of the tale!

THE LAST SÉANCE

There were four of us in the van that late October night. Philip Norwell sat behind the wheel, staring intently through the windscreen as he tried to pick out the twists and turns of the narrow road in the pale, intermittent moonlight. Tall and well-built, twenty years old, his broad frame scarcely fitted into the cramped space. Beside him, in the passenger seat, Mary Wellman sat hunched forward as she studied the map we had brought with us; using a powerful torch, she looked for the turn-off that would lead us to our destination.

I sat in the back with Andy Forrester, my legs twisted under me in an awkward position, wishing we'd brought along some cushions to help ease the growing ache in my limbs. In normal circumstances, the back of the van would have been spacious enough for the two of us to stretch out comfortably; but on this occasion there was, in addition to four small folding chairs, a large circular table which took up most of the available space.

All four of us were in our final year at university and, since our first meeting three years earlier, we had been linked by a common, and intense, interest in anything pertaining to the occult, spending occasional weekends together visiting reputedly haunted places throughout the southern counties of England, hunting for ghosts and other paranormal phenomena. Needless to say, in the large majority of cases, we had been disappointed.

When we had first started our nocturnal investigations we had applied the usual scientific methods of detection. Andy was studying electronic engineering and we usually relied on him to provide a couple of infrared cameras and other sensitive recording equipment which he claimed could pick up the sound of a pin being dropped fifty yards away.

It had been Mary who had suggested, about a year earlier, that we should perform a séance at the sites we visited.

Whether her claim to possess mediumistic talents derived from her maternal Irish grandmother was genuine or not, was something we never questioned. Fiery and quick-tempered, she was not the kind of person to cross, particularly when it came to querying her beliefs.

On the last occasion we had carried out a night-long vigil in a sixteenth-century manor house just outside Chichester which was supposedly haunted by the ghost of a grey lady and, although we had seen nothing of the apparition itself, Mary's séance had been something of a success. There had been a loud and persistent rapping on the table and twice it had moved apparently of its own volition. Personally, I was sceptical of much that happened, although I always promised to keep an open mind on the subject and to view everything objectively.

Building upon the success of our previous experiences, Andy had suggested we should visit the ruins of Elveston Abbey and carry out a séance there in the hope that we might evoke the spirit of one of the monks who had lived there before the Middle Ages. Thus we found ourselves driving cross-country at dead of night along a road that seemed pitted with potholes and determined to throw us around inside the van until every bone and muscle ached intolerably.

Breaking the silence which had lasted since we had turned off the main road some twenty minutes earlier, Philip asked suddenly: 'Are you sure we're still following the right road, Mary?'

'As certain as I can be,' Mary replied. 'But there are so many of these little country tracks in this area it's difficult to be absolutely sure. There should be a road branching off to our left about two miles further on if I'm reading this map correctly. Take that and then first right. We can't be too far away now.'

'The sooner we get there, the better,' I said, bracing myself instinctively against the swaying, jolting motion and speaking through the small rectangular grill just behind the driver's seat. 'I feel as though I haven't an arm or a leg attached to my body, cramped up in here. Everything seems to have gone numb.'

'Okay,' Philip retorted. 'We'll swap places on the way back. You can drive.'

'Shouldn't be too long now,' Mary put in placatingly. 'I'm just hoping the rain holds off, otherwise we'll be holding the séance in a downpour. I can't see there being much shelter inside the ruins.'

Easing myself forward a little, I fumbled for a cigarette, lighting it with difficulty. Over Phillip's shoulder, I could just make out a few details of the region through which we were travelling, through the windscreen. Stunted trees glided by on either side, their gaunt branches etched starkly against the sky. The moonlight was now bright enough to see a little more of the surrounding countryside. Open stretches of moorland lay on both sides and the road was a pale ribbon in front of us with deeply cut ditches bordering it. At times, something dark scuttled across it to vanish into the anonymity of the thickly tangled undergrowth and I would catch a glimpse of eyes gleaming spectrally in the headlights.

'Do we know anything at all about this place?' I asked.

Easing his legs into a more comfortable position, Andy replied: 'I looked it up in the library last week. Seems it was founded sometime in the twelfth century by members of some obscure order who came over from France. It would seem that, even from the very beginning, the brethren weren't much liked by the local people and there were a few wild tales spread abroad concerning them.'

'Maybe they extracted too much from the people by way of taxes,' Mary conjectured. 'On the other hand, the folk hereabouts would be Saxons and they'd have no love for the Normans.'

'That could be it, I suppose,' Andy conceded. 'But from what I read, I got the impression there was a lot more to it than that. According to the local legends, their beliefs deviated a lot from the norm at the time. Unfortunately any accurate records are scarce but I don't recall anything like piety in the ceremonies they practised.'

'Presumably they lost everything when Henry VIII came to the throne and pillaged the monasteries,' Philip remarked. He eased back his foot off the accelerator as a dark opening appeared on our left.

Andy shook his head. 'No, that's a funny thing. They escaped all of that and were apparently allowed to keep their wealth when almost all of the other monasteries were destroyed. In fact, if anything, they grew even richer at that time. Which suggests that they didn't exactly follow the customs of Rome. That might explain why Henry allowed them to continue.'

'There could be another explanation,' Mary interjected. 'Even in those days, Christianity wasn't as widely, or as fully, accepted as most people believe. It was only a thin veneer covering the ancient pagan religion. Who knows what terrible rites were carried out here? And like most people of that time, Henry was superstitious and although he hated the Church of Rome, and set himself up as the head of the Church of England, he mightn't have wanted to fall foul of the old gods.'

'Now you're really letting your imagination run away with you, Mary,' I told her, deliberately keeping all trace of sarcasm out of my voice. 'Besides, anything that smacked of witchcraft was mercilessly put down.'

'I'm not talking about Satanism and sorcery,' Mary declared heatedly, determined to defend her point of view. 'I'm talking about the ancient religion and that's quite a different matter.'

'Then what did happen to them?' Philip inquired.

'I'm not sure,' Andy replied. 'But whatever it was, it was pretty sudden and drastic. Piecing together what little bits of information there are, it seems that sometime during the reign of Elizabeth, all of the brethren suddenly died. Prior to that, the Abbey had been completely shunned by the countryfolk.'

'It all sounds pretty mysterious,' Philip commented, hoping to placate Mary. 'Perhaps we may uncover something really interesting this time.'

'If we ever find this place,' I put in. 'We seem to be going around in circles at the moment, getting nowhere.' Peering down at the luminous face of my watch, I saw that it was almost eleven-thirty. 'If we want to get everything set up before midnight, we'd better get a move on.'

Philip had now turned onto a track that was even narrower and more treacherous than that which we had been following. The van jolted precariously and for a moment I thought we were going to skid out of control into the nearby ditch; but somehow Philip managed to keep the vehicle on an even keel, and a few moments later Mary uttered a low exclamation and pointed off to our left. Leaning forward, I just managed to glimpse the irregular stone walls of a large ruin perched on top of a hill perhaps half a mile away.

It was soon evident that the track would not take us all the way to the ruins. Five minutes later Philip brought the van to a shuddering halt at the bottom of the hill and we all got out, shivering a little in the chill breeze that swirled in gusting eddies over the barren landscape. Here, we seemed to be miles from anywhere for, although the surrounding countryside was reasonably flat in every other direction, I could make out no sign of any human habitation in the vicinity.

'Well. Let's get started,' Phillip said

briskly. He inclined his head in my direction. 'You and Andy bring the table. Mary and I can manage the chairs.'

I threw an apprehensive glance at the sky. The moon was full, moving in and out of the scudding clouds like an animal running for cover.

A little while later, we were making our way slowly up the hillside. Here, the ground was turfy and uneven and the cumbersome weight of the table made the going difficult. By the time we reached the top, the perspiration was dripping into my eyes from the exertion.

Inside the ruins, huge blocks of stone lay where they had fallen over the centuries. The roof had long since gone, leaving the entire interior open to the sky and the elements. A brief glance was sufficient to tell me that it was not going to be easy finding a clear space where we might be able to carry out the séance. Thin streamers of mist clung around the age-old walls and there was a tangible atmosphere of utter desolation about the place that sent a little shiver of nervous apprehension through me.

116

Glancing around, I noticed that Mary had moved a short distance away and was staring about her with an odd expression on her face. She gave a slight shrug of her shoulders as she noticed me watching her and said hoarsely: 'There's definitely something here. I can feel it.'

'Ghosts of the old monks?' Philip asked.

'I'm not sure. It's a feeling I've never had before and we have been doing this for quite a while. Almost as if there is some focus of . . . *evil* . . . in this place.'

'If there is, we might be able to get in touch with it,' Andy muttered. He gave a shaky little laugh and for the first time, I realised he was more than a little scared. In all of our acquaintance, I had never known him to be the least bit afraid of anything. Certainly there was something about the ruins, a sense of unease, engendered by something more subtle, which I couldn't analyse.

Was it the way the shadows seemed to thicken and move oddly whenever the moon came out? Was it the *feel* of all those years that lay between ourselves and the time when this abbey had first been built some eight centuries earlier?

Whatever it was, it affected all of us to a varying extent, although Mary seemed the most touched by it. She stood quite still while the three of us manhandled the bulky table and chairs into position in the only clear space we could find near the northern end of the ruins.

'It's here,' she said finally in a muted, but decisive, whisper. 'Something terrible that happened a long time ago. If only I knew what it was.' She uttered a faint laugh. 'But that's why we're here, isn't it? To find out everything, if it's at all possible.' She shivered visibly and hugged her arms tightly around her body.

'You're letting the atmosphere in this place get on your nerves,' Philip said. He threw a swift, appraising glance towards the shadowed time-shattered walls. 'I think we should explore this place a bit first.'

He was already moving away before he had finished speaking, taking a torch from his pocket. I followed him a little reluctantly. Mary was right, I thought. In spite of my natural scepticism, I could definitely sense *something* — a dark, hidden menace which seemed to be growing more pronounced with every passing second.

Ahead of me, Phillip played the beam of the torch over a huge stone slab. The moon had temporarily vanished behind a bank of dark cloud but by now my eyes had adapted to the darkness and it was easy for me to pick out details. A massive arch, still mainly intact, reared up in front of us and, in spite of the iron rein I had on my emotions, I could not suppress a shudder as I passed beneath it. The wind, blowing up the hillside, made eerie, whistling sounds among the stones like a lost voice calling out a warning down the centuries. My mind was curiously alert now, attuned to any manifestations which might take place, or any unnatural emanations the place might be giving off.

Edging round the stone slab, I bumped into Philip, who had halted suddenly. He edged back a couple of paces, taking hold of my sleeve and pulling me with him.

'What's this?' Bending, he flashed the torchlight along the stone. 'There are some inscriptions here.'

I went down on one knee beside him, grabbing at his shoulder for support. The incised symbols were very faint, scarcely visible. Weathering had worn much of the stone almost smooth but from what I could make out, they were clearly old Saxon miniscules and not the usual Latin normally found in religious places.

'What do you make of them?' Philip asked, crouching down beside me and running his fingertips over the stone.

'It's clearly Saxon,' I said. 'But don't ask me to read any of it.'

'But why Saxon? These were Normans who came here.'

'Have you found something?' Mary had come up and was peering intently at the slab.

'Could be,' I replied. 'But I'm dammed if I know what it means. I always thought these religious orders invariably used Latin but this is undoubtedly old Saxon. If this order did originate in France, why on earth would they use this language? It doesn't make sense.'

'Particularly if this happens to be the

altar stone,' Philip pointed out. He straightened up.

'I think we should make a rubbing of it,' Mary said. 'We may be able to get a translation of it later. Someone at the university may know enough old Saxon to give us the gist of what it says.'

'There's a job in front of us then,' Philip said. 'But I guess it'll be quicker and more accurate than trying to write it down.' He glanced at his watch, then at Mary. 'You want to try the séance first? It's almost midnight.'

Nodding, Mary led the way back to where we had left the table and chairs and a few moments later we were seated with our hands resting lightly on the table, our little fingers and thumbs touching in a circle. When we had done this on previous occasions, I had treated it as little more than a harmless joke, not expecting anything dramatic to happen. Certainly there had been times when the atmosphere inside some empty building had been undeniably conducive to something abnormal occurring. This time, however, was different. There was undoubtedly something about our surroundings, some indefinable aura emanating from these ancient stones, which made me oddly tense. Overhead, the moon had now broken free of the clouds and its yellow light threw long grotesque shadows over us as we sat in taut silence, our eyes fixed on Mary's face.

'Are we all ready?' she asked in a low voice.

The three of us nodded in unison. Then Andy said hoarsely: 'I'm not sure we should be doing this. This isn't like those other places we visited. I've got the feeling that there's something really evil here.'

'If you're scared, you don't have to stay,' Philip said sarcastically. 'You can go back to the van and wait for us there.'

'Is that what you want to do, Andy?' Mary asked.

After a brief pause, I saw him shake his head uncertainly. 'I'll stay,' he muttered. 'But I still think we should be careful.'

'Then let's get on with it.' Mary straightened in her chair, staring straight ahead. 'If there is anyone here, please communicate with us.' Her voice was low, yet it seemed to echo eerily as if the ancient stones had somehow amplified it and thrown it back mockingly at us.

Nothing happened and Mary repeated the words, speaking a little louder this time then, suddenly and without any warning, the heavy table gave a violent jerk under our hands. At the same time, the air became appreciably colder, sending shivers through my body.

In almost the same instant, Mary abruptly stiffened in her chair. Seated beside her, I sensed her entire body go rigid as an iron bar. Her head was thrown back so that she appeared to be staring directly into the sky above the roofless ruins. The muscles of her neck were corded with the strain. I knew at once that she was not feigning this curious attack.

On more than one occasion, she had appeared to go into a trance but I had put it down to theatrics, hoping to make others believe in her talents. Now I was not so sure. Something seemed to have taken possession of her.

'What's happening?' Philip asked in a low murmur.

'I'm dammed if I know,' I answered.

'Do you think we should try to snap her out of it?' Andy muttered.

'No!' Philip's denial was sharp. 'If she is in a trance that could be dangerous.'

A moment later, a new phenomenon manifested itself. There was a sound like confused whispering in my ears; very faint, just at the limit of audibility, and with a twinge of fear, I realised that the whisperers were very close and all around us.

Though the bright moonlight proclaimed that, apart from the four of us, the ruins were empty, they seemed undeniably thronged with a multitude of invisible shapes, all whispering and murmuring ceaselessly within the dark moon-thrown shadows!

'Do you hear it?' Andy twisted his head violently to stare around him. 'Voices. All around us.'

'It's nothing more than our imagination,' Philip retorted, evidently struggling to remain calm. 'Nothing but the wind among the stones.'

'I don't think — ' I began, then stopped.

124

Mary's head jerked forward. A string of harsh, guttural syllables came from her mouth; uncouth words in a language none of us recognised. Yet even though their meaning was unknown to any others, there was an undertone of menace and evil that shocked us deeply. The torrent of words went on for over a minute before Mary suddenly slumped forward over the table, her head on one side, her eyes closed.

Breaking the circle, I caught her by the shoulders and pulled her gently back into the chair. Her face was icily cold under my fingers; her breathing was harsh and irregular as if it was an effort to force air into her lungs. After a few moments, however, her eyes flickered open. For a second, they refused to focus on me. Then, with a shudder, she relaxed slightly, reaching up and grabbing my arm in a tight, convulsive grip.

'God! That was awful.' Somehow she forced the words out through tightly-clenched teeth. 'Something had hold of me. Something black and formless. What happened while I was under?'

'You started speaking in some weird language,' Philip told her. 'We couldn't make any sense of it.'

'And there seemed to be voices murmuring all around us,' Andy chipped in.

'This isn't like the other times we tried this.' Philip turned his head slowly, staring into the long grotesque shadows. 'They were all pretty tame compared to this. I don't reckon we should try anything else. We'll make that rubbing and then get the hell out of here.'

Helping Mary to her feet, I supported her for a minute or so until she had regained something of her former composure. The experience had clearly shaken her to the core and, as she moved away from the table and into the flooding moonlight, I noticed how white and drawn her features were, how her eyes kept twitching nervously, her gaze flicking in all directions.

Ten minutes later, Andy had made a rubbing of the inscription around the altar stone. Rolling it up carefully, he took it down to the van before returning to lend a hand with the table and chairs. And all the time, we had the unshakeable impression of being watched — of *something* scrutinising us from somewhere within the shadows.

Not until I was seated in the driving seat beside Andy, with Philip and Mary now in the back of the van, did I allow myself to relax a little. The experience had been more unnerving than any of us had expected.

It was Philip who broke the uneasy silence. 'Whatever happened in there, it's something I never want to go through again. It's no wonder those superstitious peasants shunned the abbey all those centuries ago.'

'Well I, for one, am glad we are away from it all,' I said. 'At least, we didn't conjure up any material manifestation. Had we, I think I'd have made a run for it.'

'Me too,' Andy said out of the corner of his mouth. 'If those tales they tell about these ruins are anything to go by, I'd say we got off pretty lightly.'

Settling myself more comfortably into

the hard, metal driving seat, I gave a nod of agreement. But what I didn't know, what none of us knew, was that the real horror was only just beginning.

* * *

Mary was the first. It was two weeks after our nocturnal visit to Elveston Abbey when I bumped into Andy in the cloisters at the university. I could tell at once by the expression on his face that something was wrong.

'Have you heard the news about Mary?' he asked.

I shook my head. 'No, what's happened?' I had no idea what was coming but, even at that moment, I had the feeling that it was something really bad. I hadn't seen Mary for three days but had assumed she was busy getting prepared for the exams which were coming up soon.

'She was taken home yesterday.' There was a faint tremor in his voice. 'I don't know many of the details. It all happened so suddenly. She hadn't been feeling too well for a couple of days but yesterday morning, she became much worse. Some kind of fever, they reckon. Her room-mate told me she had wakened during the night with Mary moaning and muttering something about a black shadow in the room.'

'A black shadow?' I repeated. 'Sounds to me as though she was delirious. I just hope it's nothing serious. She was looking forward to coming with us on our next trip in three weeks.'

'We may get to know something more tonight. I have let Philip know and he's going to ring her parents to inquire about her.'

I knew that Philip had met Mary's parents on a couple of occasions and, in spite of my immediate concern for her, he was the logical one to approach them for more information. Also, since my room was adjacent to his, I decided to drop in on him that evening and try to be present when he phoned. Whatever the reason, I had the strongest feeling that there was more to Mary's sudden illness than met the eye. At the time, however, I did not connect it with our nocturnal vigil at Elveston Abbey.

It was a little after seven when I knocked on Philip's door. He answered it almost at once and ushered me inside. Once we were seated, he said: 'Has Andy told you about Mary?'

'Yes. I saw him this morning. Does anyone know what's wrong with her?'

'Not really. I was just going to ring her parents when you knocked.'

'Do you mind if I wait?'

He shook his head. 'Not at all. I'll try to get as much information as I can. I tried to get something out of the doctor here this afternoon but all he would say was that she developed a high temperature and some kind of rash. She's certainly feverish; possibly some virus she's picked up.'

He went to the phone in the hall, leaving the door open. I could just make out his voice a few moments later and guessed that he had managed to get through. He spoke for several minutes, then came back, closing the door quietly behind him.

'Well?' I asked when he didn't speak.

For a moment, he stared at me across the table and it was as if I didn't exist. Then he pulled himself together. 'Mary's been rushed to hospital. They don't think she'll pull through.'

'Good God. Do they know what it is?'

'They've no idea. At first, they thought it might be meningitis but they've carried out tests and that's been definitely ruled out. This is something else but it's got the doctors baffled. Apparently they've tried antibiotics but none had any effect. Whatever it is, it's bloody deadly.'

'If it turns out to be contagious, perhaps the whole university may have to be given protective shots.'

'Goddamnit! That wouldn't do any good if they don't know what it is.'

'But there must be something we should do,' I retorted. 'God knows how many people have been in contact with her over the past couple of weeks.'

'All we can do is wait and see if there are any more cases. If even one shows up, then the medical authorities will know what to do and we'll hear about it soon enough.'

I made to say something more but at that moment there came a knock on the door and Jenny Winthrop, Mary's roommate, looked in.

'I just dropped by to see if you've had any word about Mary,' she said.

Philip motioned her in. 'It's not good news,' he told her. 'Frankly, they don't think she'll last the night.'

Jenny sank into one of the chairs. 'I keep thinking about her, about those strange things she said.'

'What sort of things?' Philip asked.

'Oh, I don't suppose they mean anything. I reckon she must have been raving at the time. At first, I didn't take much notice. She kept insisting there was a shadow following her wherever she went. It would be in the corner of the room but then it would gradually get closer. At night, with the light on, she used to sit in her chair at the table, just staring at the wall.'

'Did you see anything?' I asked.

I saw her hesitate, as if unsure how to reply, then, moistening her lips, she said in a low voice: 'It was nothing more than my imagination, of course. It couldn't have been anything else. She'd been going on about it for so long, I must have half-expected to see something. But a couple of nights ago — ' She broke off sharply, shaking her head slightly.

'Go on,' I insisted. 'Anything you can tell us might be important.'

'Well . . . I'd been in the library until quite late and I'd just got in. I remember she was standing in the middle of the room, her back to me, staring at nothing. I thought maybe she hadn't heard me and I didn't want to startle her because she'd been quite jumpy of late, so I coughed to attract her attention. But for more than a minute it was as if I didn't exist. Then she turned and, honestly, I've never seen such a look of absolute terror on anyone's face before. She pointed to the far wall and said, 'There! Do you see it?' At first I didn't know what she meant but then I saw what she was pointing at. Her own shadow was there on the wall but just to one side of it, there was another. It wasn't very distinct. The impression I got was that of a bent, hooded figure. It could have been anything, of course. Yet even though I looked all around the room, I couldn't see anything there which could have cast that shadow.'

I felt a little shiver pass through me at Jenny's words. There had to be some logical explanation, I told myself. Some ornament in the room, perhaps, which had cast a distorted shadow of itself upon the wall. It was very easy to assign a weird shape to something that bore no actual resemblance to the object casting the shadow.

I returned to my room five minutes later with my thoughts in turmoil, struggling to make sense of what I'd heard. More and more, I was coming around to the inescapable conclusion that what had happened to Mary was, in some way, connected with our experience that night at the abbey. Was it possible that we had, somehow, evoked a malign spirit of one of the old monks? Insanely, the idea occurred to me that we were now paying a terrible price for meddling with things that should have been left alone.

I went to bed early that night. I was very tired, yet I did not sleep as soundly as I had hoped, for no sooner did I fall asleep than I had a most disturbing dream. I stood within the confines of Elveston Abbey but not in its ruinous form as I had last seen. This was the place as it must have been many centuries earlier and all about me, in the fitful glare of several large candles, stood a multitude of dark, cowled figures. From somewhere in the distance came the sound of chanting, and my sense of horror was increased by the realisation that this was no normal religious service which was being held — for the words were uncouth gutturals, similar to those which Mary had uttered while she had been in that trance.

As I watched, the surrounding shapes moved together into a form of procession and I had the impression of being elevated high above the throng until I seemed to be looking down upon the scene from somewhere near the high roof. At the head of the column I saw a half-naked figure struggling in the grasp of two of the monks; and at the northern end of the building, where the huge arch stood, was that hideous altar stone I had seen in waking life with those black forms standing behind it, one of which held a long-bladed knife balanced across his outstretched hands.

I knew then what I was witnessing, just as I knew with a sick certainty that what Andy had discovered about Elveston Abbey was undoubtedly true. Those brethren had brought no wholesome religious doctrine with them when they had come to these shores from France eight centuries ago. The ceremonies they had performed all that time ago had nothing to do with the Christian faith.

In the refectory the next day, I found Philip and Andy together and deep in serious conversation. As I sat opposite them, Philip said solemnly: 'Did you sleep well last night?' Before I could give him an answer, he went on: 'Neither Andy nor I did and it turns out we both had essentially the same nightmare.'

'Being inside Elveston Abbey in the old days?' I said. 'Seeing that hideous sacrifice?'

'That's right.' There was a note of undisguised surprise and tension in

Andy's voice. 'And yet just before I woke, there was the conviction that someone — or something — was aware of me, stalking me through the building and down the hill. I couldn't see it. I couldn't even tell where it was but it was there, not very far from me.'

'But what does it all mean?' Philip interrupted. 'Surely three people don't have the same nightmare on the same night? That's stretching coincidence a little too far.'

'If it isn't coincidence, it has to be something else,' Andy said. He put a hand to his head and rubbed his forehead gingerly. 'But I'm damned if I want to think about what it might be.'

There was an awkward pause and I sensed that all sorts of wild ideas were going through my friends' minds. Hoping to instil a little calm and reason, I said: 'My guess is that all three of us have been badly affected by what's happened to Mary and we are subconsciously associating it with what happened that night.'

Philip gave an emphatic shake of his head. 'I don't believe that for one minute.

All right, maybe you'll both think I'm crazy but I think that place is evil; that something terrible was done there centuries ago and it's still there. Mary sensed it the minute we went inside the room. She said there was a focus of evil there and I believe she was right.'

'And you're saying that it's followed us?' Andy's face twisted into a grimace of consternation.

'I think that before we all start to imagine things, it might be better if we wait until you get a translation of that Saxon inscription,' I put in. 'That might tell us something. Does anyone know what happened to it?'

Philip fumbled in his jacket pocket and brought out a slip of paper. 'I took it along to Professor Wainwright to see if he could make anything of it. I didn't tell him where we made it. However, he managed to make a rough translation of the symbols.' Handing it to me, he went on: 'I don't know what to make of it.'

Smoothing out the sheet on top of the table, I read what the professor had written: *As in Egypt, the Lord sent plague to destroy utterly those evil ones who set themselves up against His holy ways.*

'A plague!' Andy exclaimed. 'Then you don't think that — ?'

'Now hold on a minute,' I interrupted quickly, guessing at his thoughts. 'Just because of mention of a plague, that doesn't mean we have to jump to the conclusion that Mary's got some unknown infectious disease from just going to that place. Anything like that would have died out ages ago. And if you read your Bible you'll find there were several different plagues mentioned. It could have been anything.'

Philip stared across at me and managed a ghastly grin. 'There was something else on that rubbing we made. Professor Wainwright feels certain that this inscription — ' he tapped the piece of paper with his forefinger, ' — was added sometime during the Middle Ages by one of the village folk and after all those monks had mysteriously died. There was a much earlier inscription on the stone but it had been almost completely defaced.'

'An earlier inscription?' Andy repeated.

Philip bit his lower lip, then said: 'We

were right when we figured that block was the original altar stone. It was probably brought over by the monks from France eight centuries ago and the professor believes it was some invocation to the pagan god. When this catastrophe struck the abbey sometime during Elizabeth's reign, the villagers ransacked the place and destroyed everything in it. But they couldn't destroy the altar stone so they erased what was on it in the first place and then added this later writing.'

Andy opened his mouth to say something more but at that moment Jenny Winthrop came hurrying over and from the expression on her face I knew that something terrible had happened. She sank into the chair next to me.

'Mary's dead,' she said harshly. 'I've just heard. She died in hospital early this morning.'

The skin on the back of my neck was suddenly tingling uncomfortably. I didn't know what to say. Philip mumbled something under his breath and then lapsed into an awkward silence.

When we broke up a few minutes later,

Andy said: 'Will you try to find out when the funeral is, Philip. I'd like to go.'

'I'll let you know,' Philip promised.

But as events transpired he never kept that promise, for that was the last time either of us saw Andy Forrester. In retrospect, I suppose I must have sensed how ill he was that morning in the refectory, how he kept putting up his hand to his head as if it pained him. Some time that afternoon, he was rushed into hospital in Oxford with a raging fever, raving and screaming about a shadow which followed him wherever he went, drawing ever closer.

The following morning he was dead and, as in Mary's case, it appeared that the doctors had no idea what had killed him. That was when Philip and I became really scared. Mary's unexplained death might have been put down to something she had contracted anywhere but I could not convince myself that Andy had simply caught it from her. I only knew that I had the feeling that somewhere a terrible evil had been unwittingly unleashed by our actions that night — a blight from long ago which had now claimed two victims and was, even then, moving remorselessly in our direction.

The following week passed without any further incident. Both Philip and I were busily engaged preparing for the exams and there was little time in which to think of the tragic and bizarre events that had happened since our visit to the abbey.

Then, early one evening, there came an urgent knock on the door of my room and, opening it, I found Philip standing outside in an extremely agitated state. I made him come inside and sit down. It took several minutes for him to calm down sufficiently to be able to speak directly, and at the end of that time he seemed more ashamed of his manner than ready to speak openly of its cause. But I was determined to get to the bottom of it and insisted that he should tell me what was wrong.

'All right,' I said firmly as he sat nervously on the edge of his chair. 'What is it?'

'Oh, come on, Steve,' he retorted, 'you know damned well what it is. It's happened twice before and now it's happening to me.' He ran the back of his hand across his forehead and I noticed he was sweating profusely. 'And don't tell me it's just my imagination or a coincidence. I've seen it for myself. Just occasionally at first, but it's all the time now, wherever I go, and coming closer every hour.'

'What's there?' I demanded harshly, exasperated by his rambling talk.

At that, he rose unsteadily to his feet, swaying a little, one hand grasping the edge of the table. 'Look for yourself if you don't believe me.' Turning slowly, he pointed towards the wall near the window.

For a moment, I thought that the strain of preparing for the coming exams had affected his mind.

And then I saw it!

The electric light was behind us, throwing our shadows onto the wall. But there was undeniably a third shadow there, one that was certainly cast by nothing I could see in the room! It was, perhaps, six inches from Philip's; oddly indistinct, yet bearing a certain resemblance to a crooked figure, shorter than our own, warped and bent almost double like that of an old man.

'What in God's name is it?' Somehow, in spite of the fear that constricted the muscles of my throat, I got the words out in a hoarse croak.

'It's what Mary and Andy saw before they — ' He deliberately left the remainder of his sentence unsaid but I knew what he was alluding to. After several seconds, he went on, speaking slowly and deliberately. 'I noticed it a couple of days ago but thought nothing of it, thinking it was just a trick of the light. But it's gradually getting closer to my own shadow.' He drew in a deep breath as if to steady himself, and let it out slowly. 'Move away from me towards the other side of the room. You'll see what I mean.'

Wordlessly, I did so, watching my own shadow move with me.

After a brief pause, Philip edged slowly sideways, past the small table. The ghastly shape moved with him.

'Now do you see?' Hysteria tinged his voice. 'We conjured up something during that séance, something unutterably evil. Now it's come after us. We should have guessed it. The old peasants believed that God sent a plague to destroy those monks for their blasphemy — and it's true. They wrecked the building but they didn't destroy whatever evil entity it was those monks worshipped. That's remained there all these centuries until we went and meddled with it. Now we are paying for it with our lives.' His voice rose to a short crescendo as I attempted to calm him down.

'This is all pure conjecture,' I said fiercely, struggling to force evenness into my tone. I knew that at the first sign of panic on my part he would crack completely and there would be no handling him. Already, he seemed on the verge of complete mental collapse.

'I'll get you into bed,' I said firmly. 'What you need is a good night's sleep. 'We'll talk about this in the morning.'

'Call it conjecture if you like,' he muttered almost inaudibly. 'But you can't convince me. I know what it is. Just as surely as I know that once that goddamned shadow touches mine, I'm finished.'

Taking him tightly by the arm, I led him back to his own room. As I made to switch on the light, he stopped. 'I'll manage all right in the dark,' he said thickly.

'Okay,' I said, knowing what was in his mind; that in the darkness there were no shadows.

Somehow, I got him into bed, fully clothed, for he was still shuddering violently and, although most of his body was icily cold, his forehead was burning. As my eyes grew accustomed to the darkness, I noticed that his were wide open, staring wildly into the corners of the room but after a while, he fell into a restless sleep and I left, closing the door softly behind me.

Two hours later, I looked in on him again, taking care not to turn on the light. There was no movement as I approached the bed but I could hear his harsh breathing. Feeling his forehead, I found that he was even hotter than before and I decided to call the doctor.

He came about fifteen minutes later and while he examined Philip, I stood at the end of the bed, unable to take my gaze from the grotesque black shadow which stood out starkly on the pillow just beside my friend's head. I couldn't call the doctor's attention to it, or even try to explain it to him. Not even when the ambulance arrived and Philip was carried on a stretcher from the room and downstairs with that malignant shape following him all the way, was I able to say anything.

I stayed at the hospital for a couple of hours after he had been admitted, drinking cup after cup of black coffee from the vending machine in the waiting room. When the doctor came out, I inquired about Philip's condition, only to be told that he was stable for the moment but still giving rise to concern since all attempts to bring down his dangerously high temperature had so far proved unavailing.

After giving particulars of Philip's next of kin, I said: 'This is some kind of new fever, isn't it, doctor? One you've never come across before.'

He gave me a queer look. 'Why do you say that?'

'Because it's struck twice before. Two of my friends died recently from the same thing — and now he's got it.'

'I see.' The doctor rubbed his chin

thoughtfully. 'And do you have any idea where the three of them might have contracted it?'

I shook my head. It was, of course, impossible for me to tell him the truth; he would not have believed it, would almost certainly have thought I was insane. 'Not really. All I know is that their symptoms were identical to his and none of the antibiotics they tried had any effect.'

The doctor jotted down something on his pad, then said: 'Well, we'll keep him under observation during the night. By tomorrow morning, we should know something more definite. In the meantime, I suggest you go back to the university and get some sleep.'

★ ★ ★

It was with a curious mixture of dread and anticipation that I stretched myself out on my bed and tried to will myself to sleep. Such terrible, inexplicable things were happening that it was impossible to compose my floundering thoughts sufficiently for sleep ever to come again.

148

Finally, however, I must have fallen into an uneasy doze for, again, I had that hideous nightmare — of hanging suspended somewhere above the interior of Elveston Abbey and seeing that monstrous procession moving slowly towards the altar. This time, I recognised the half-naked struggling figure, saw the white fear-contorted face staring up in my direction.

It was undeniably Philip, his lips drawn back across his teeth in a ghastly rictus of absolute terror. And there was something more in that great, open space — a *Thing* almost completely concealed within the shadows beneath the arch. It was not human, nor animal; a huge, atramentous shape, crazily indistinct, with red gleaming eyes, that slowly edged its way forward, inch by inch, so that I knew that, within moments, it would emerge from the darkness and come into full view.

Then the nightmare helplessness which gripped me like a vice, making it impossible to move or cry out, suddenly broke and I yelled aloud and I woke, shivering uncontrollably, jerking upright in the bed.

Now the horror in my mind was

unequivocal and not to be denied. I knew with a sickening certainty that Philip was dead, and that the curse — or whatever it was — which we had inadvertently brought upon ourselves by that injudicious séance had drawn three of us into its dark web of death.

I knew also, that the end was very near for me.

★   ★   ★

This morning, making my way through the cloisters, I happened to turn my head and there, not far behind me, was a second shadow, which followed my own!

SOMEWHERE A VOICE
IS CALLING

Away from the main state highway, the Louisiana countryside takes on a wild and sombre aspect. Here there are narrow roads, twisting and treacherous, with deep ruts and large boulders littering the surface, making driving difficult. Seldom do the county working gangs come to this isolated region to make any repairs; and the heavy storms have eroded the shoulders away so that, in places, the road surface vanishes into the encroaching swamps.

There is also something disquieting in the way the deserted and ruined farmhouses seem to hide themselves away in the folds of the hills with their densely wooded crests, as if having no wish to be seen by the outside world. Here there are creaking wooden bridges, which span deep gorges where dark and turbulent streams run swiftly and no hint of sunlight ever reaches. Any unwary traveller forced to negotiate these roads after darkness has fallen literally takes his life in his hands, coming unexpectedly upon diabolical hairpin bends between age-old trees that blot out most of the sky.

But very few people use these old roads now. Most of the original French settlers have gone, drifting away to the towns, and it has been left to a handful of property developers to move in and set up some cabins for city folk to come on vacation.

It was to one of these that I drove late one spring night. It was the end of the semester at the small university where I taught ancient history and I had promised myself a short vacation in this region for a couple of years but, until then, the opportunity had never presented itself.

The road I was travelling was narrow with tortuous climbs and sharply angled bends. Had there been any other traffic on the road, it would have been physically impossible for two vehicles to pass since the erosion had been exceptionally bad in this region. By now, it was almost dark and I was forced to switch on the headlights to pick out the numerous obstacles that littered the surface. In one place, the shell of a dead tree had fallen directly across the road, blocking it completely, and I had been forced to stop the car, get out, and manhandle it out of the way before being able to proceed any further.

I had passed a number of empty cabins along the way, searching for the small group of freshly painted buildings which the owner, a Philip Denzer, had assured me in his letter were readily visible from the road. I had also been given to understand that a number of other visitors were present on the site and, if I arrived after dark, the lights would mark it out quite distinctly, even though it was set back some distance from the road at the end of a short side trail.

I was barely crawling now, for the road was so twisted that the probing headlights penetrated only a few yards into the deepening dusk before they were completely swallowed up by the dense growth of trees lining the road and forming a barely distinguishable dividing line between it and the deadly swamp on either side. I seemed to have been on this road for hours and uncertainty was growing in my mind, the conviction that I must have missed the turn-off in the darkness; and my apprehension was compounded by the knowledge that it would be utterly impossible to stop and retrace the route.

Then, swinging the car precariously around a bend, I just caught sight of faint yellow lights gleaming through the trees a short distance away to my right. A few moments later, the headlights caught the gap where the trail branched off the road. Turning the car onto it, I eased my foot off the accelerator, leaning forward to peer through the dusty windscreen, trying to pick out details in the gathering gloom.

Fortunately, the trail led straight ahead and finally led me into a large clearing with perhaps a dozen cabins ranged around the perimeter and a large building, which I took to be a small general store and the place where Denzer lived. There was the moist earthy smell of the swamp in my nostrils as I parked the car in front of the store, got out, and stretched my cramped legs. A couple of other cars stood outside the nearby cabins, two of which had yellow lights showing through the curtained windows.

There were also lights in the lower windows of the two-story building; and going inside, I found Denzer, a man in his mid-fifties, seated at a table. On the long shelves around the walls were stacked various items of merchandise while outside, I had noticed a large tank which I guessed contained kerosene for use in oil lamps which, out in the wilderness, would be the only source of illumination. It would be many years, if at all, before the county got around to bringing electricity to this desolate out-of-the-way region.

Denzer got sharply to his feet as I entered. 'You'll be Doctor Enfield,' he said. 'Expected you a couple of hours ago but I reckon you ain't used to these roads. I've got your cabin all ready for you.' He shuffled towards a wooden key rack that hung lopsidedly on the far wall. 'If you need anything for eating tonight, I've got most everything here and there's a stove in the cabin.'

'I had something to eat before turning off the highway,' I told him. 'I guess I'll manage until morning.'

'Suit yourself.' He took down a key and preceded me to the door. I expected him to accompany me to the cabin but instead he stood just outside the doorway and I noticed that he had his head cocked on one side as if listening intently for something. Thrusting the key into my hand, he gestured along the parking lot. 'Third cabin along,' he said hoarsely. 'I hope you enjoy your vacation here.'

As I brushed past him, he muttered harshly: 'Just one thing I should warn you about. I tell it to all the guests. Being a city man you won't know much of these parts. I wouldn't go prowling around after dark, especially any distance from the parking lot. It's easy to get lost out there and there are gators in the swamps. You wouldn't be the first to just disappear.'

'I reckon I know better than that,' I replied. I could fully understand the dangers of wandering around this place in the darkness, yet there was something in his manner that struck me as distinctly peculiar. Whatever it was, I couldn't quite put my finger on it, but he gave me the impression that he, too, was scared of something out there and it wasn't just the presence of alligators.

As I made my way to the cabin after taking my things from the car, I heard music coming from the one next to mine and glimpsed an occasional shadow across the curtained window. At least, I reflected, I might have a little company during my stay. I didn't relish having just the strange owner as my sole companion. Even on so short an acquaintance, I sensed there was something odd about him, although at the time I put that down to his living out here in the midst of all this desolation, seeing only the few visitors who came. Later, I was to discover the real horror that lurked around this locality.

The cabin was in good condition and clean, with sturdy wooden steps leading up to a long veranda resting on stout wooden supports driven deep into the soft earth. Inside, I lit the two lamps I found on the table. The furniture was undoubtedly cheap, but serviceable, and the bed looked comfortable. There were a couple of chairs and, out on the veranda, a large rocker.

After taking stock of everything I went outside and lit a cigarette. At the moment I did not feel the need to sleep. The strain of driving along that treacherous road had left me tense and restless. Settling myself into the rocking chair, I put my feet up on the low wooden railing, and sat listening to the sounds of the night. Here, the quietness of the place was vastly different to that in the town. There was a soft whisper of the breeze in the trees, the rustle of unseen things in the matted undergrowth, and an occasional splash from the direction of the swamp.

After a time, the music from the next cabin stopped, the lights went out, and I guessed the folk there had retired for the night. At some point, I must have fallen asleep for when I next came to full awareness, I felt cold and there was a strange trembling in my body as if I had just woken from some forgotten nightmare.

Something had woken me; some unexpected and unusual sound which had intruded upon my sleeping mind. Sitting upright in the rocker, I peered into the surrounding darkness. It was then that I became aware of the sound. It was just at the limit of audibility but it stood out starkly from the other nocturnal noises, which had been present before I had fallen asleep. As I sat there, listening, it seemed to grow louder and more distinct, as if the source was approaching me — a human voice forming inarticulate words although I could make no sense of them. The sound was so unexpected that I rose from my seat and walked down the veranda steps and crossed to the far edge of the parking lot where the trees and bushes shrouded the periphery of the swamp.

I had not been mistaken. The voice undeniably came from that direction, yet I could think of no one who would be out there in the middle of that deadly morass.

It was too dark to make out anything

159

and the only conclusion I could reach which might logically explain the voice was that the natives of this region still put their boats out into the swamp at night, possibly for fish. But if they had been calling to one another, surely there would have been two or more voices, whereas I felt certain there was only one. A lonesome sound echoing in the darkness.

Flicking my lighter, I held it so that I could see the face of my watch. It was a few minutes after midnight. Leaning forward, I tried to pick out the sound of a paddle but there was nothing to indicate the presence of a boat nearby. The cry came again, even closer now — but still there was nothing visible.

Then there was silence. Never had I thought that silence could be so deep, even out here in the midst of the swamps. The small, tiny sounds I had heard before falling asleep were gone. Only an odd breathless hush lay over everything.

When it became clear that the sound was not going to be repeated, I returned to the cabin and it was just as I paused in front of the steps that a sudden movement caught my attention.

A face had appeared at one of the windows on the upper story of the store. So someone else had heard the voice, I thought, and a faint shiver went through me as I recalled the way Denzer had stopped in the doorway in an attitude of listening. Had it been him standing at that window, staring out into the night? Furthermore, was it that voice which he had been warning me about and not the danger from the alligators?

Puzzled, I went inside, locking the door behind me. Turning down the lamps, I undressed and stretched myself out on the low bed. Whether it was because I had already slept on the rocking chair, or being in a strange place, I couldn't decide, but I found it difficult to fall asleep. There was something about this place that niggled at my mind, throwing up a multitude of questions and speculations. There was no doubt that Denzer was mortally afraid of something out there, yet I had no idea what it could be.

The following morning I woke with a dull ache behind my eyes. I had hoped to sleep for hours after all that driving on the previous day, but several times during the night I had wakened, finding myself subconsciously listening for any repetition of that strange voice. But there had been nothing beyond the normal nocturnal sounds.

In one of the cupboards I found a set of pans and five plates, two large and three smaller ones, while there was also a drawer full of cutlery. Enough for me to cook some food over the stove, I decided, feeling a sense of adventure which I had not experienced since the days I had spent in the Scouts many years before.

The sun had come up some time earlier, though it was still hidden behind the tall trees which fringed the site and the air still held a trace of the night's chillness. Leaving the cabin, I walked along to the store, pushing open the door, which creaked protestingly on rusted hinges. Denzer was standing behind the low counter reading through a dog-eared book. He glanced up as I entered and eyed me shrewdly.

'You're up early, doctor,' he observed. 'Sleep all right?'

'Not really,' I replied. 'Kept waking up nearly every damned hour. The change of scenery, no doubt. Do you have any aspirin?'

'Sure thing.' Turning, he rummaged along one of the shelves. 'Anything else you need?'

I reeled off a list of the items of food I required and waited while he got them and placed them on the counter.

'If you ever feel like having a meal here, my wife can always rustle you up something,' he said genially. 'Save you preparing it all yourself. Several of the folk who come here do that when they don't feel like cooking it for themselves.'

'I'll probably take you up on that sometime,' I said, placing the items in the large bag he provided. He now seemed disposed to talk and my purchases led to a rambling conversation.

Denzer had bought this place some eighteen years before, being originally from Ohio. During the late spring, summer and autumn months there were enough visitors to keep him busy. But in the winter, he shut the place up for four or five months. He could go back to town during that off period but he preferred to stay and carry out whatever repairs might be needed, although he admitted there had been times when the storms were pretty bad and it had proved impossible for him to get through to town for more provisions.

While he had been talking I noticed the woman who had come down the stairs and was now moving unobtrusively around at the far end of the room. I judged her to be no more than twenty, dark-skinned, and clearly a native of this region. Since he had made no mention of having a daughter, I wondered if this could be his wife. To me, it seemed odd that a woman as young as this, possessing a certain beauty, would fall for a man more than twice her age. I knew that customs among the primitive people of this backwater were far different from those in the more civilised regions, but surely there must be men of her own age she could have married instead of this far older man.

Still, I figured it was not my business if

she chose to spend her life with a man old enough to be her father.

It was as I left with my groceries that I bumped into an elderly couple, who had evidently just come from the cabin adjacent to the store.

'You'll be the visitor in Cabin Three,' said the man, stretching out his hand. 'I'm Jim Wakefield. My wife Lottie. I expect we'll be seeing quite a lot of each other in the next fortnight.'

Shaking hands, I introduced myself, asking: 'Is this your first visit here?'

'Good Lord, no,' Lottie replied, shaking her head. 'We have been coming here every year about this time for the past fourteen years. Wouldn't go anyplace else. So peaceful and quiet after New York.'

'Then you must know Mr. Denzer pretty well. What kind of man is he?'

Her husband shrugged his shoulders in a noncommittal way. 'We have always found him to be friendly enough, willing to do whatever he can for you. If you ever need anything, you've only to ask and he'll fix it.'

I thought of mentioning the voice I had

heard calling from the swamp but I suddenly felt unsure of myself. Instead, I said: 'The young woman I just saw in the store, who is she?'

'You mean Roxanne,' Lottie answered. 'She's Mr. Denzer's wife — his second wife to be precise.'

'I see. Have you any idea what happened to the first?'

'Nobody knows. It happened a year ago, shortly before we arrived. Rumour has it that Eloise just upped and left him.' Lottie seemed anxious to impart this little bit of gossip although I couldn't fail to notice the warning look her husband flashed at her.

'Probably she didn't like living in this place,' I suggested. 'After all, I guess it must get pretty lonely, especially during the winter when everything is closed up.'

Jim shuffled his feet nervously for a few moments, throwing a quick glance in the direction of the store. Then, lowering his voice a little, he murmured: 'Some reckon that Denzer was seeing Roxanne for some time before Eloise left. Can't say whether there is any truth in that. Roxanne's a

166

swamp-girl, that's what they call the natives of these parts. Only about fifteen when she came to help in the store. There was another odd thing that happened, as I remember. It was about a year back. Roxanne disappeared shortly after she and Denzer were married. Some say there was evidence of some kind of struggle there and the general opinion is that her folks hadn't taken too kindly to her marrying him and that they'd broken into the store one night and taken her back with them while he was lying in a drunken stupor upstairs. Anyways, she turned up again less than a week later, though we both noticed how she'd changed.'

'In what way?' I asked.

'She was such a lively, vivacious child before that,' Lottie put in. 'Though it was clear she'd got her hooks into him not long after she came and was determined to marry him once her chance came. She used to sing the old Creole songs all day long but now she seems just like a shadow of her former self. She moves around the place so quietly you'd hardly notice she was there.'

'And no one knows what happened to Eloise?' I enquired, by now quite intrigued by this news.

Jim scratched his cheek. 'Denzer won't talk about it much. As for the idea that Eloise hated this place, we know for a fact that isn't true. She loved it, even more than he does, used to spend a lot of her time with the swamp folk. Had a boat tied up yonder — ' He jerked an arm in the direction of the edge of the parking lot, ' — and used to spend most of the day out there. I don't hold with the notion that she just left. I reckon there's a lot more to it than that.'

'You think she may have found out about his affair with Roxanne?'

'Well, if she did, she gave no sign,' Lottie interrupted. 'But take my word for it, there's a mystery here.'

'Perhaps I'll try to get to the bottom of it before I leave,' I said, half-jokingly.

Jim looked serious as he said: 'I wouldn't joke about these things if I were you. Bad things happen down here and the folk don't take too kindly to outsiders like us prying into their affairs.'

He looked so much in earnest that I gave a quick smile. 'Don't worry, I'll be very discreet. Somehow, I doubt if there's anything sinister going on.'

After cooking myself some breakfast on the stove, I decided to make some explorations of the area. I had long been fascinated by the legends and customs of the early settlers in this region and, since today promised to be fine and warm, this seemed the opportune time to do it.

Denzer was standing on the stoop of the store when I went out, staring towards the swamp, a queer expression on his face. It cleared a little as I approached.

'I'm thinking of taking a look around the swamp,' I said. 'I'd like to talk with some of the people in the area. Can you tell me the best way to reach them?'

'The swamp folk?' he said. 'Why do you want to talk to them?'

'I'd like to get to know something about their history and customs,' I explained. 'That's part of my work at the university. If I can obtain some idea of their folklore at first hand, it would be extremely useful in my research.'

Denzer shook his head. 'You'll be wasting your time,' he declared decisively. 'They don't talk with strangers. I've been here a long time and very few of them ever come here except for a few supplies. They don't even like us being here.'

'Perhaps so. But I intend to try,' I answered.

He kept silent until I began to wonder if he meant to ignore my question completely. Then he pointed off to the right. 'Do you know how to handle a boat?'

When I nodded, he went on: 'You'll find one over there. Go upstream for about a mile or so until you come across a narrow tributary on your left. Follow that for maybe half a mile. You might find some of them there. But be careful how you go. The gators don't often attack boats but they've been known to do so and I wouldn't answer for the consequences if one did.'

Thanking him, I walked to the end of the clearing where he had indicated. Here the ground became more marshy and my shoes sank into the brown ooze. Some twenty yards further on I came upon a short anchorage with a couple of boats tied up to long poles. Stepping into one, I took the two oars after untying the rope and tossing it into the bottom of the boat. It was several years since I had used a boat but I soon found that my old skills had not deserted me and I was soon moving out into the deeper water.

By now the sun was high in the sky and still it was hot and humid. Low overhanging branches, thickly festooned with wiry vines and other creepers, impeded my initial progress, but in a few minutes I came out into more open water where a wide channel led inland. There was barely any current and I was forced to use the oars strenuously to propel myself upstream, struggling to keep the flimsy craft in clear water. Twice I glimpsed something large which gave rise to a narrow, triangular wake but although one of the alligators ventured dangerously close to me, for the most part they seemed content to sun themselves on the mudbanks, completely ignoring my presence.

Very soon I was perspiring freely with the heat and the exertion of rowing through the sluggish water. By the time I came within sight of the narrow tributary that Denzer had described, it had seemed more like ten miles than one since I had left the landing site. Now my progress became more difficult. It was impossible to tell how deep the water was, but the surface was clogged with long weeds and greenish scum and there was the cloying stench of rotting vegetation, which caught the back of my throat.

The threadlike channel twisted tortuously through shallow banks of sneaking roots where they had intertwined and grown together to form an almost solid mass of living plant tissue. In places there was barely sufficient room for me to use the oars but finally, rounding a bend, I glanced over my shoulder and made out a collection of crude wooden huts, which seemed to be standing on the water.

As I edged nearer I saw that this was, indeed, the case. Each building had been erected on thick wooden piles driven deep into the mud. A number of people were in evidence as I somehow drove the boat against a rickety landing stage. Looping the rope around a pole, I clambered up onto the broad planks. There was something menacing in the stares I received and a faint tremor of apprehension seized me as I walked towards the small knot of men.

'You lookin' for somethin', mister?' muttered one of the men ominously. The accent made his speech almost unintelligible.

'I'm trying to find out something of the history of this region,' I said, forcing evenness into my tone. From the attitude of the men surrounding me, I had the feeling that my position was precarious. 'I'd also like to know if any of you are in the habit of going out onto the swamp at night.'

As I asked my question, I noticed how the man's expression suddenly changed. At first, he had regarded me with naked suspicion and hostility but this look had instantly altered to one of fear.

'Nobody goes into the swamp after dark,' he insisted finally. 'I reckon you'd better get back into your boat and go back to wherever you have come from. We don't want you here and — ' He broke off quickly and turned his head sharply. A voice had come from within the nearby hut. The words were harsh and authoritative but spoken in some local dialect I did not understand.

Before I could make a move, the man stepped forward and grasped me tightly by the arm, propelling me towards the entrance of the hut. The doorway was so low that I was forced to bend my head as I was unceremoniously thrust inside.

For an instant, panic seized me. Denzer had warned me against going into the swamp. Did these people intend to murder me and throw my body into the water where it would never be found? Already, I was beginning to regret the rashness of my action in coming here alone.

Inside the hut it was so dark that I could make out very little. The man pushed me down into a chair, then turned on his heel and walked out without a word.

Slowly, my eyes became accustomed to the gloom and I looked about me, not knowing what to expect.

Then the voice came again and I made out the figure lying on the bed against the wall. It was impossible to gauge the age of the woman who lay there but I had the impression that she must have been a hundred years old. The lined wrinkled face was brown and leathery but the eyes, fixed intently on me, were bright and intelligent. Her voice, though thin and reedy, possessed a strange resonance.

'You came here because of something you heard, isn't that right?' she asked harshly. 'You came from Denzer's place along the river.'

I admitted that I was, indeed, staying at the site and that I had fancied I had heard a voice calling from somewhere in the swamp on the previous night.

'Ah, I could tell. I know much of this man, Denzer. He is evil, but soon he will know the meaning of vengeance.'

'What do you know of him?' I asked as she uttered a cackling laugh that sent a shiver along my spine.

'I know enough, believe me. I know how he treated his first wife and then took one of our kind in her place. But we have our ways of exacting retribution.'

I felt my flesh beginning to creep as if I were in the presence of something uncanny, which I could not understand. I wanted to get out of there but what little I already knew of the strange affair made me curious to learn more.

'I can understand his wife leaving him once she found out about his affair with Roxanne,' I said quickly. 'But — '

'Leave him!' The older crone cackled again. 'You know nothing of what happened. She never left this place!'

There was such vehemence in the woman's voice that I knew, instinctively, that she spoke the truth.

'Eloise is still here?' Somehow, I got the words out.

'Oh, yes. She's here, all right. And she'll never leave until Denzer has paid for what he did. There was murder committed here nigh on a year ago.' Her voice dropped a little in volume and a skinny claw raked the air in front of her face. 'We have strange ways here which no one from outside knows anything about; nor would they believe them if they did.'

I was beginning to feel distinctly uneasy. The gloominess inside the hut and the aged crone's wild statements were having that effect on me. Already, a horrible suspicion was beginning to form in my mind.

'You're not talking about voodoo, are you?' I asked, struggling to keep my emotions under tight control.

Again there was that harsh, high-pitched laugh. 'Voodoo? No, mister, this ain't voodoo though there may be those who don't know the difference. But we believe that a murderer can control the ghost of his victim, making it do anything he commands. But I've said enough. If you wish to know more, listen for that voice. It will come again — and then you will know.'

'Know what?'

'What happened a year ago — and who that voice is calling to. Now go!'

I realised she would tell me nothing more, yet what she had already told me had started a train of thought in my mind that would not be stopped, that led me to only one conclusion. Either Denzer had killed his first wife, or he and Roxanne had planned and executed it together and her body had been disposed of in the swamp where it would never be discovered. I did not doubt that this was what she had meant when she had stated so emphatically that Eloise had never left.

Yet all of my scientific training rebelled against the notion that it had been Eloise's ghost I had heard the previous night, calling from the swamp, although I was convinced that it had been a woman's voice I had heard.

Leaving the small settlement, I made my way quickly back downstream, plying the oars mechanically as I attempted to think clearly and logically. I had never believed in the existence of ghosts, yet there was something here that seemed unexplainable in rational terms.

As I tied the boat to the pole I noticed a figure standing some fifty yards away. It was Roxanne. She had her back to me and appeared to be staring intently at something beyond the trees. Her whole attitude was puzzling and it was several seconds before I recognised where I had seen that same pose before. Denzer, standing in the doorway of his store, his head held to one side, listening to something I could not hear!

Very quietly, I walked to the end of the stone jetty where a fringe of trees hid me from her view. A sudden sound reached me from the direction of the cabins and, glancing round, I noticed that a young couple had emerged from the cabin next to mine and were standing on the veranda, talking loudly. Looking back to Roxanne, I saw her attitude had not changed; she seemed to be totally oblivious to everything going on around her.

For the space of perhaps five minutes she stood there, absolutely motionless, her gaze fixed on something invisible to me. Then she gave a quick, but distinct, nod of her head, turned, and walked back to the store, moving like someone in a trance, looking to neither left nor right. Climbing the wooden steps, her legs moving swiftly and jerkily like a puppet dancing on invisible strings, she went inside, closing the door behind her.

I spent the remainder of the day trying

to piece together the little strands of information I had gained, hoping to form some reasonable picture in my mind. When looked at objectively, very little of it seemed to make any sense. After all, what did I know? Both Denzer and his present wife were acting extremely odd, as if there were something in the swamp they were both mortally afraid of. The aged crone had spun me a rambling tale of murder and the ghostly possession that could have been a complete fabrication.

There remained only that voice I had heard calling from the swamp in the middle of the night. How much of that was nothing more than my imagination? I wondered. After all, I had just woken from a deep sleep and for all I knew there were certain animals or birds that could closely imitate a human voice.

For the next three days I lazed around the site, once walking along the narrow road for perhaps a couple of miles to get some idea of the overall layout of the area. I saw little of Denzer or Roxanne during that time, nor was there any repetition of that voice although, for some reason I could not quite analyse, I deliberately remained awake every night, sitting out on the veranda until well past midnight, unconsciously expecting to hear it calling out of the darkness.

On the afternoon of the third day, I was sitting in the rocker on the veranda sipping a cold beer when Jim Wakefield came over and stood leaning against the railing, resting his weight on his elbow. I could tell at once that he had something on his mind which he wished to confide to someone.

After a long pause he threw an uneasy glance in the direction of the store where Denzer stood in the doorway, and said in a hushed voice: 'Have you noticed anything odd about our host while you've been here?'

'Odd?' I asked. 'In what way?'

Wakefield paused, then went on: 'He seems to have changed completely since we were here last year. There's something about his manner which I don't understand. Stays inside the store all the time as if he's scared to come out. And he's always — '

'Listening for something?' I finished.

'Why, yes. That's it exactly.'

I hesitated for a moment, then asked: 'That first night I arrived, did you hear anything — around midnight?'

Wakefield thought for a moment, then shook his head. 'Nothing out of the ordinary. Why do you ask?'

'Because I could swear I heard a woman's voice calling from out there in the swamp.'

He shook his head in obvious bewilderment. 'But that's impossible. What on earth would anyone be doing out there at that time of night? Unless it was Roxanne. She's one of those people, you know. She knows the swamp like the back of her hand. But why she should be out there at midnight, I've no idea.'

'It could have been her, I suppose,' I answered. That was an explanation I hadn't considered. 'But there's more to it than that.' Briefly, I told him what I had learned from the old woman. He listened in silence until I finished.

'You're saying that Eloise was murdered by her husband?'

'It's possible. You told me yourselves how much she loved this place, so why should she leave? Do you think she was the kind of woman who would have simply walked out and given him a divorce so that he could marry a girl half his age?'

Wakefield pondered that for a few moments, then gave an emphatic shake of his head. 'We got to know Eloise pretty well over the years we've been coming here. She was certainly a very strong-willed woman, stubborn, not the kind to submit meekly to what was clearly going on. She'd put quite a bit of money into this place, far more than he did. I can't see her just storming off and leaving it all behind. Believe me, she'd have wanted her share before she'd agreed to divorce him.'

'And as far as you know, she never came back? You never saw her again?'

'Never.'

Getting up from the rocker, I walked down the steps and stood beside him, aware that Denzer was watching us curiously from the doorway. Quite suddenly, the perspiration was chill on my body. 'Then my guess is that the old

183

woman was speaking the truth.'

'And you reckon it's Eloise's ghost you heard calling from the swamp?' Wakefield's face had suddenly assumed an ashen colour.

'To be quite honest, I don't know what to think. I've tried to go over everything in my mind but it always comes out the same. I've never believed in ghosts or the occult, or voodoo for that matter, but right now, I'm not sure of anything.'

* * *

By evening, the air had grown heavy and oppressive and there was no doubt that the pleasant weather of the past few days was coming to a dramatic end. There were dark, ominous thunderheads building up on the horizon presaging a storm. Not even the slightest breath of air stirred the leaves on the nearby trees and a deep, expectant hush lay over the swamp.

Normally such storms moved in pretty quickly but this one was different. By the time it grew dark, it still hadn't broken. Perspiration dripped into my eyes as I went outside the cabin and lowered myself into the rocking chair. It was far too hot and sultry to remain inside, yet even in the open, there was little relief. I knew there would be no welcome coolness until the storm had passed.

Lights burned in the store and the other two cabins but I hadn't put out lamps, preferring to sit in the darkness. I felt strangely tense and apprehensive and knew that my growing alarm had nothing to do with the approaching thunderstorm. It was something more than that; the feeling that something terrible was about to happen, yet I had no idea what it might be, nor from which direction it would come.

The first vivid lightning bolt was a vicious streak of blue-bright fire which must have struck somewhere within a quarter of a mile of where I was sitting, for it was followed almost immediately by a savage roll of thunder that hammered concussively at my ears. Scant seconds later, large, heavy raindrops began to fall and within seconds the downfall became torrential — an almost solid wall of water, so dense I could scarcely make out the far perimeter of the parking lot. The drumming on the roof of the cabin became a continuous roll of sound.

More lightning flared and to my bemused mind it seemed that the storm was centred over the nearby swamp and that, oddly, it was scarcely moving. I had experienced several storms like this in the past, but this one was different from anything I had previously known. All of the others had been accompanied by gale-force winds, and once I had been caught in the middle of a hurricane in Florida when it had swept in from the Atlantic across the coastline.

But here there was no wind. The air was absolutely calm with the rain coming straight down, turning the parking lot into a quagmire. From my vantage point, I could make out occasional dark silhouettes against the curtained windows in the two neighbouring cabins and I guessed that the occupants were watching the vivid lightning display just as I was. Then, a little after ten-thirty, the lights went out in the windows and I reckoned they had retired for the night. Lights still burned on the upper windows of the store, however, and I knew that Denzer and his wife were still awake.

Then, just after midnight, the thunder and lightning ceased. It was not a gradual diminution in the ferocity of the storm but an abrupt cessation, such as I had never experienced before. Everything stopped; the rain halted instantaneously as if someone had shut off a tap and a deep unnatural silence settled over everything. The transition from the tumult of the storm to such absolute stillness was so unexpected that I started up from the rocker and leaned forward, grasping the wooden rail tightly with both hands.

All around me, the air seemed charged with electricity so that my flesh tingled uncomfortably and the small hairs lifted on the back of my neck.

For what seemed an eternity, the silence persisted. Then, from somewhere in the distance, I picked out the eerie sound I had heard a few nights before. I recognised it instantly as a woman's voice, coming closer from the direction of the swamp. The words were unintelligible, but there seemed to be a terrible meaning behind them, which made me shiver convulsively, the knuckles standing out whitely in my fingers as my grip tightened on the railing. Suddenly, I had the impression that something was wrong — *terribly* wrong.

Desperately, I tried to make out anything that moved beyond the fringe of trees; but there was nothing.

How long I stood there, staring wild-eyed into the darkness, it was impossible to tell, with that weirdly echoing voice calling endlessly in the night. Then, without warning, there came another sound; another voice, raised in mortal terror. It came from the store and, almost without realising it, I had jumped down the veranda steps and was running through the ankle-deep mud of the parking lot towards the building. Even as I reached it, the sound was abruptly choked off by a ghastly gurgle and then there was silence. Even the voice from the swamp had dwindled into a death-like hush.

The door of the store was locked but a

few moments later Jim Wakefield came running up and together we broke the door from its rusted hinges.

'What the hell's going on?' Wakefield gasped as we stood inside.

'I've no idea,' I told him, 'but it sounded like Denzer's voice up there.'

There was now utter silence inside the store as we ran towards the stairs, taking them two at a time. At the top I paused, looking around me. There was a short corridor with two closed doors along it, one on either side. Motioning Wakefield towards the nearer of the two, I ran for the other, thrusting it open with my shoulder.

The room was lit by a single kerosene lamp on the small bureau and by the steady yellow gleam I witnessed a terrible scene. Denzer lay on the long bed, his body contorted, arms and legs twisted unnaturally on the crumpled covers. Crouched over him, her hands clenched tightly around his throat, Roxanne stared at me across his body. There was something about her eyes, dead and vacant, which held me rooted to the spot, unable to move a muscle until Wakefield crashed into me from behind. Dimly, I heard his sharp intake of breath as he stared over my shoulder.

'Dear Lord in Heaven.' He muttered the words in a horror-filled voice.

One glance was sufficient to tell us that Denzer was dead, the life throttled out of him. His tongue protruded from swollen lips and his eyes stared sightlessly at the ceiling. But it was as I moved slowly forward towards Roxanne that the real horror occurred. I had taken only a couple of faltering steps, eyes fixed on her totally emotionless face, when her outline shimmered strangely. Within seconds, she was gone, fading swiftly like smoke.

It was in that mind-numbing instant that I saw everything; how utterly wrong I had been in my initial assumption. Eloise had not been murdered. She had deliberately planned all of this from the beginning. Undoubtedly, her knowledge of the old ways of the swamp folk and her friendship with them had enabled her to carry through her diabolical plan to perfection.

It was she who had come back from her

hiding place in the swamp a year earlier and had entered the store while her husband lay in a drunken sleep, creeping upstairs to kill Roxanne and carry her body away to dump it in that morass of mud and ooze. When Roxanne had apparently returned a week later, oddly changed as the Wakefields had attested, it had been merely the dead shell of the girl, a walking corpse activated and controlled by Eloise's will, just as the old crone had told me.

Now that her work was done, Roxanne's spirit had returned to its final resting place somewhere deep within the ooze. Somewhere out there, I thought, Eloise was standing, watching the store, aware that her revenge was now complete. There would be no more voices calling through the night. The deed was done.

I knew it would be impossible for Wakefield to believe what I knew to be the truth. That something supernatural had happened he was unable to deny, having witnessed it with his own eyes.

I also knew that I could not stay and face Eloise Denzer when she returned to claim what was now hers, which she undoubtedly would, for there was no jury on earth who would believe my story were I ever to tell it.

Leaving that room of horror with Wakefield close on my heels, I hurried back to my cabin, packed my things, and got in the car, preferring to take my chances with the treacherous roads and the darkness than remain another hour in that accursed place. The final revelation, the ultimate confirmation of my fears, came as I drove out of the parking lot and accelerated the car along the short track leading on to the winding road.

As if Denzer's death had been a signal, the storm broke again with an appalling suddenness and, just as I swung the car onto the uneven road, a white figure appeared briefly in the glare of the headlights — a woman's form moving purposefully towards store. I had just a brief glimpse of the white face twisted into a leering expression of triumph and, in my ears, a voice was calling the words in an alien tongue, a hideous sound which echoed even above the crash of the thunder rolling across the berserk heavens!

THE DARK THRESHOLD

Hidden away in the southwest of England, on the border between Cornwall and Devon, lies a small hamlet called Morwenith. It stands miles from anywhere, isolated from its neighbours by rough country and low domed hills where, at intervals, one comes across long-abandoned cottages, still crudely thatched and empty, the gardens untended, their rotting woodwork bleached white by the sun. Nonetheless, despite its isolation, it was there I went during the summer of 1989, having stumbled upon the village during a walking holiday three years previously.

In particular, I had been much taken by a large rambling house half a mile north of Morwenith. Then it had lain empty and there had been something about it that had immediately taken my fancy. Now, three years later, I had purchased it, much to the obvious amusement of the villagers who regarded me as mad for wanting to live there. The house was undoubtedly very old, dating back to the mid-seventeenth century but still in excellent condition.

Considering the price I was asked, I felt sure I had got a bargain; but on quizzing Mrs. Goad, who agreed to come in for four days each week to clean for me, the reason I had obtained it so cheap was due more to its reputation than its age and comparative isolation.

'Are you trying to tell me that there's some local superstition regarding this place?' I asked, the first morning she mentioned it.

'Not superstition, sir,' she replied. 'But hard fact. Many folks hereabouts believe it to be haunted.'

'Indeed, and by whom?'

'Well, sir, the story is that about two hundred years ago, the younger mistress of the house got tired of her husband's inattentions and took a lover from the village. William Malmesly was the husband's name, a very wealthy man in those days. Anyway, the wife and lover conspired to murder him and one night the wife let the lover into the house and while she remained downstairs with her maid, the lover crept up to the master's room, burst in and stabbed him through the heart. They tried to cover up their crime, of course. Later that night, when the servants were all asleep, they carried the body down to the wood yonder and buried him by the lake. Next morning the lover dressed himself in the husband's clothes and rode off quickly in full view of the servants while Charlotte Malmesly put it around that he had been called to London on urgent business and would not be returning for several months.'

'And did they get away with it?' I enquired.

'That I don't know, sir. But as far as the villagers are concerned, there is one thing they are certain of. William Malmesly's spirit is definitely earthbound. Not that I've ever heard anything in this house, otherwise I wouldn't be here now, believe me.'

'Well, I doubt if I'll lose any sleep over these tales,' I told her. 'To my knowledge there are hundreds of houses where people have died by violence and the more ancient the building, the more likely you are to have such stories spread abroad.'

Mrs. Goad picked up my empty teacup. She looked distinctly uncomfortable, head bent, studying the cup and saucer in her hand. 'Unfortunately, that isn't all, sir. Like I said, I don't really believe in them myself. It's my conviction, as a God-fearing woman, that the dead remain dead until Judgement Day but — '

'Go on, Mrs. Goad,' I urged when she showed no sign of continuing. 'What more is there?'

'Well, if you must know, there was a gentleman who stayed here about seven years ago. Like you, I think he preferred peace and quiet. A writer of some sort, he was. I used to look after him as well. He hadn't been here long when he started imagining things.'

'What sort of things?'

'He wouldn't say, sir. But I noticed at times that he would be talking to me, quite naturally, and then he'd stop quite suddenly and his eyes would be looking at something, as if he was following someone moving around the room but, of course, there was no one there.'

'As if there were some other person in the room which only he could see?'

'That's it exactly, sir. It used to give me a queer turn whenever it happened, I can tell you.' She drew in a deep breath, then went on: 'That went on for some months and then, one morning, I came in just as usual to find him gone. He'd vanished as if the floor had opened and swallowed him up.'

'There's probably a logical explanation,' I assured her. 'Maybe he'd finished whatever he was writing and gone back to town without telling anyone.'

'No sir, that weren't it.' Mrs. Goad shook her head vehemently. 'All of his things were left, nice and tidy, as he always kept them. There was even a half-finished page in his typewriter.'

'Strange,' I conceded. 'And were the police informed?'

'Oh, yes. Right away. They had search parties out looking for him but they found nothing. He just . . . disappeared.'

'And it's believed that his ghost haunts this place?'

Mrs. Goad forced a faint smile. 'Lord, no sir. Not him. Wherever he went, I'm sure he's at peace.'

'So I only have the ghost of William Malmesly to worry about,' I said light-heartedly.

'It isn't wise to mock these things, sir,' Mrs. Goad admonished. 'There are things which are beyond our understanding; things which are best left undisturbed.'

I could see that she was deadly serious and decided to drop the subject, leaving her to get on with her work while I made a round of the house, checking for any sign of rot in the woodwork. There was clearly quite a lot to be done before the house was fully habitable. The large front room was still in a state of good repair as were the kitchen and three of the upstairs rooms, one of which I had furnished as my bedroom and another as a library for my book collection.

For a fortnight my work was totally taken up by renovations to the remainder of the house. Since few of the villagers would enter the place, let alone work on it, I was forced to engage workmen from

Plymouth — five stolid and unimaginative men who knew nothing of the local lore concerning the house and would probably have given it little credence if they had.

It was during the course of this restoration work that I discovered the manuscript, which, if the contents are genuine, not only confirmed many of the spectral tales spread around the village, but completely changed all of my previously held ideas and beliefs regarding the supernatural.

The large front room had evidently served as a banqueting hall during the early decades of the house's existence. In the centre of one wall stood a large open fireplace, clearly the original, and as such I intended to restore it to its former splendour.

On either side, carved stone pillars supported an equally splendid lintel decorated with curious motifs. It was as I moved my fingers over the carved nymphs and satyrs that I touched some concealed protuberance. There was a soft click and a portion of the lintel slid aside, revealing a dark cavity. Brushing away the accumulated dust, I probed inside, my fingers closing around something that felt like a notebook. Drawing it out, I studied it carefully.

The pages were brittle and yellowed with age, all filled with a neat and legible writing. Here and there the ink had faded a little, but fortunately no moisture had got to it. I guessed it to be between one and two hundred years old yet, on glancing briefly through it, I noticed one extremely odd fact: the style of writing and the words used were far more modern than the age of the manuscript would indicate.

Although highly excited by my find, I put it to one side, determined to read through it that evening when I would have far more time to digest its contents fully and without any distractions. The remainder of the day was taken up with supervising the work on the building and it was not until late that evening that I took up the manuscript and settled myself into a chair to read the strange and frightening tale which I now set down in the hope that some reader may find some explanation for what, to me, is utterly inexplicable.

★ ★ ★

'My name is Paul William Stanmore, or at least that was a name I was given at birth. Now I am not sure of anything anymore. Everything that has happened is either a nightmare from which there is no waking, or I am going insane. Whatever it is, I must record everything as it occurred in an attempt to preserve my sanity and leave a permanent record. I have already discovered the secret compartment in the lintel above the fireplace and once my account is finished, I shall endeavour to place it there in the hope that, in some future year, someone may find it and know what really happened in this accursed home.

'The old house had lain empty for close on seventy years before I moved in on 23rd of January 1982, and for a couple of centuries at least it has had an evil reputation. As a result, I got the place for a ridiculously low sum. The strange stories which were rife in the village made no impression on me, certainly not sufficient to deter me from living here. As a writer of horror fiction, the place was ideal; well away from any external distractions and providing just the right atmosphere for my work.

'Most of the ancient furniture, although dilapidated, was quite serviceable and, since my needs were extremely basic — although the lack of electricity was a drawback — I soon settled in. Despite the nature of my writing, I am not a superstitious man; but within a few weeks of moving in I ceased to deny that odd things happened in this old house — things I could not rationally explain.

'I had, of course, heard some of the stories concerning William Malmesly, murdered by his wife's lover in 1747, and the belief among the villagers that the place is haunted. The former I soon ascertained to be historical fact but the latter I instantly dismissed as nothing more than idle gossip such as is inevitably attached to many old houses, whether they deserve such a reputation or not.

'My first intimation of something strange within the house occurred about a week after moving in. Prior to that there had been nothing out of the ordinary. That evening, having finished my usual meal, I was seated at my typewriter when I heard faint sounds coming from the far corner of the room where the candlelight from the table failed to penetrate. My first thought was that there were rats in the wainscoting, scratching away at the ancient woodwork. Then, as I listened more intently, I seemed to make out human voices, nothing more than disjointed sentences, uttered so low that the words were indistinguishable, being just at the limit of audibility.

'The sounds continued for perhaps ten minutes before fading away completely. Telling myself that it had been nothing more than my imagination, I forced myself to concentrate on my writing, occasionally listening for any further repetition of the sounds, but there was nothing.

'As the days passed, I became increasingly more convinced that I must have either imagined it all, or had subconsciously put human speech to normal, nocturnal noises within the house.

'A fortnight later, however, I heard the voices again, still little more than a muted whispering from which it was difficult to pick out any intelligible words. On this occasion, they were in the corridor just outside my bedroom door. I had gone to bed that night with a pounding headache, due no doubt to having spent more than four hours typing by the flickering light of the candles. The pain was still there, just behind my forehead when I woke from a brief doze. A glance at my watch told me it was a little after two-thirty. The house was very still and there was no wind whining and moaning around the ancient eaves.

'This time I was just able to distinguish two voices, those of a man and a woman; and from what I could hear, they appeared to be arguing violently. Cautiously levering myself out of bed, I moved silently to the door and stood with my ear pressed against it but without being able to make out anything but a few occasional words.

'On the bureau beside the door stood a tall brass candlestick, which I seized before pulling open the door.

'The corridor was empty!

'Thoroughly shaken by my experience, I returned to my room and sat down on the edge of the bed. I could no longer doubt that there was something supernatural in the house. After a while, I grew calmer. Whatever it was, it had shown no maleficent action towards me and I finally decided that, in the morning, I would investigate this thing further.

'The next day, I went down into the village and sought out the Reverend Bannister who, I had been told, was a local authority on the history of the village. He seemed to know the whole story but it was difficult to tell how much he was willing to impart for his answers to some of my questions were curiously evasive. In the main, his accounts were similar to that which I had already heard from some of the villagers. James Undershaw's ruse in passing himself off as Charlotte Malmesly's husband had succeeded in allaying any suspicion for several months but when William had not returned from London after almost a year, rumours began to spread through the village and Undershaw's increasingly frequent visits to the house did not go unnoticed.

'Queries in London yielding no knowledge of William Malmesly ever having arrived there, soon led the authorities to commence an inquiry into his whereabouts and his remains were eventually discovered in the wood. Undershaw was hanged for his murder and Charlotte was imprisoned as his accomplice.

'While he was only concerned with the historical facts of this case, and did not believe in the spectral tales muttered about in the village tavern, Bannister did admit that, on one occasion, after arriving home late at night, he had passed the empty house and had seen a flickering yellow light gleaming through one of the lower windows. At first, he put it down to light reflecting off the glass but, in retrospect, he was certain that the moon had been hidden behind the clouds at the time.

'When I mentioned the curious sounds

I had heard, his demeanour changed abruptly. Gravely, he told me that it was his considered opinion that houses such as this could get to certain people, particularly those who had any dealing at all with the occult. He even suggested that perhaps it was my writing of horror stories that had contributed to my hearing these things, and somehow it had attuned me to the correct wavelength for receiving such impressions.

'Whether or not this was the case, over the ensuing weeks, the manifestations continued. I would hear the disembodied voices in many parts of the house but, as time passed, I realised that the voices appeared to become louder and more insistent in the long upper corridor, becoming more distinct with each night. Furthermore, I soon found it possible to distinguish among the different voices. One was undoubtedly that of a young man, generally in conversation with a woman. At times, I had the impression that, if I were to turn quickly enough and glance in the right direction, I would be able to glimpse the speakers.

'This situation went on for almost two months, by the end of which time I ascertained two facts about the whispers. From certain of the phrases which I was able to pick out, these ghostly presences belonged to some time at least a couple of centuries in the past, a discovery which confirmed that, somehow, I was overhearing conversations which had taken place among the family who had lived there about the time of William Malmesly's death. In addition, I felt sure that, by some psychic means, I was actually immersed in the plot which had led up to his slaying; that all of this was being enacted precisely as it had all happened all that time ago. I could even identify the two central characters by their voices: James Undershaw — the murderer and lover of William's wife — and Charlotte Malmesly herself. The other voices I heard at various times, usually downstairs in the kitchen, were undoubtedly those of the servants of the time.

'Curiously, these ghostly events did not frighten me as much as I would normally have expected. I had taken this house in the hope that the atmosphere prevailing inside the place would be conducive to my work and enable me to meet the deadline set by my publisher. Strangely, I now found it easier to concentrate on my writing, with the words flowing smoothly from my brain onto the typewritten page.

'I had no idea how long these manifestations would continue, whether they would finally culminate in the actual murder itself and then end — or whether they would repeat themselves endlessly like a film running continuously.

'I was not, however, prepared for what came next. It was an evening in mid-March when the next phase began and the element of true horror first intruded into my senses. It had been a blustery day, typical of the month, with brief sunny spells and heavy showers coming up with the wind from the southwest. I had intended going into the village for some supplies during the morning but the inclement weather forced me to put off my trip until later that afternoon when the weather cleared a little. Accordingly, it was growing dark by the time I returned.

'As I turned into the narrow lane I noticed a faint light in one of the bottom windows. It was not a steady gleam as I would have expected from the lowering sun glinting off the windowpane. Rather this was a flickering glow such as would come from a candle or the fire in the hearth. Yet I knew I had left no candle burning and as for the fire, that had already blown down to a few embers when I had left.

'Puzzled, I made my way quickly to the door, unlocked it, and went inside. The large front room seemed just as I had left it. Only a faint red glow came from the fire, certainly not sufficient to have given the impression I had noticed from outside. It was then that I looked towards the table. Faint spirals of smoke rose from the two candles. They had both been lit and then snuffed out the instant before I had entered the room!

'My first coherent thought was that someone had seen me leave an hour earlier and was still in the house. A thorough search of all the rooms, however, revealed no one, nor had anything been disturbed.

The back door was securely bolted on the inside and it would therefore have been quite impossible for anyone to have slipped out of the house without my seeing them.

'Since there was no logical explanation for what I had observed, I tried to put it out of my mind as I prepared a meal and then settled down for a further stint at the typewriter. Outside, another storm had broken. The rain lashed the windows curiously, while the wind howled around the eaves like a banshee.

'For a little while nothing untoward happened. Then, out of the corner of my eye, without looking up from the type-writer, I noticed that the flames of the candles were slowly changing colour. The wan, yellow glow now shone with a ghastly greenish lustre, giving the objects within the room a hideous appearance; and the shadows behind the table and in the far corners held a darker depth of blackness. I had been considerably taken aback when the candle flames had changed, but had thought it due to some impurity in the wax which would soon right itself. But when this did not happen, I began to feel the first twinge of real fear, a sensation of impending horror.

'Then, in the corner of the room where the stairs led up to the upper rooms, two dim shapes slowly materialised, mere hazy outlines of a man and a woman, standing close together and speaking in low tones. That these were the figures of the main characters in the ghostly drama, which had previously only been played out aurally, I could not doubt.

'After several minutes, during which I sat transfixed at the table, the woman moved away, vanishing through the door which led towards the kitchen while the man drifted slowly up the stairs; and, as my bewildered gaze followed him, I thought I glimpsed a long-bladed knife in his hand.

'Scarcely had the shape disappeared at the top of the stairs than the candle flames resumed their normal glow. Sitting back in my chair, I realised I was shivering and sweating at the same time. Had I simply imagined all of this? Was it possible I been working too hard, often well into the night, that I was beginning to see things? Or was I really witnessing events that had occurred more than two centuries earlier?

'Nothing further happened that evening and I retired early, more shaken by my experience than I cared to admit. Even before I had heard those first whispers in the rooms and corridors, I had been vaguely aware of something unseen, yet definitely present, in the old house. Now, I was beginning to see things.

'That night I took a couple of sleeping tablets, hoping to sleep through until morning; but in spite of this, when I woke suddenly from a dreamless sleep, it was only a little after two. At first, I could not identify what had woken me. The house was very quiet. Outside, the storm passed and there was a deep hush over everything. Then, as before, I picked out the low murmur of voices immediately outside the bedroom door. On this occasion, I remained where I was, afraid that if I opened the door I might come face-to-face with those wraiths I had seen earlier. After a little while, the voices fell silent. There was a faint creak of footsteps moving away along the passage.

'By now, my senses were sharpened to

such a pitch of preternatural sensitivity that I knew that only one person had moved away. The other still remained in the corridor.

'With an effort, I forced myself into an upright position on the bed, staring through the enveloping darkness at the door. A few moments later, there was the unmistakable sound of the knob being turned, followed by the creaking of hinges as the door was thrust open.

'Yet, to my straining vision, the door remained closed!

'There came the sound of approaching footsteps drawing nearer to the bed, menacingly stealthy steps. A dimly visible shape advanced through the darkness, the substantial figure of the man I had seen earlier, the knife held in his upraised hand.

'Heart-stopping terror held me immobile on the bed. Then, even as the knife flashed downwards towards my chest, the apparition vanished. The room was empty!

'I should have left that accursed place the next morning. I had seen and heard enough to convince me that something terrible had taken place there two centuries earlier and the evil echoes of that deed still lingered within the house. Had I done so, the ensuing horror would have been averted and I would not be here now, waiting for the terrible and inevitable ending of this drama.

'What kept me there, despite my natural fear, was perhaps the thought that I might be able to carry out a scientific investigation into all that was transpiring, and maybe incorporate it into one of my books.

'By now, it was becoming increasingly clear that there was a certain progression as far as the events were concerned. First, barely audible whispers in certain parts of the room, then the voices becoming plainer and stronger, until I was able to distinguish whole sentences and now, visual apparitions. Just where would it all eventually lead? That was what I was determined to find out.

'Over the following three weeks the hazy, indistinct figures grew more and more discernible. At the same time, I found myself noticing other aspects of the house were slowly changing. At first, it was as if there were two overlapping images in front of my vision. Initially, these were only brief flashes of a second seen intruding upon my sight. The dim image of a chair in the corner of the large room where no chair existed. A large portrait above the wide hearth where a mirror actually hung.

'As the days passed, however, the shadowy panorama became increasingly more real and the familiar surroundings of the house diminished. It was as if I was becoming more than a casual spectator of the dramatic events which were now unfolding from the house; that I was somehow being drawn into them, leaving my own time behind and going back through the years to the actual time of the murder.

'Nightly, as the ghostly figures became more and more substantial, I was witnessing the same sequence of events. Coming from the direction of the kitchen, Charlotte Malmesly would hurry to the back door, letting in James Undershaw, and together they would plot the slaying of her husband. First they would stand in the large banqueting room and then in the long corridor upstairs where she pointed out her husband's bedroom to her lover. After they returned downstairs, they engaged in further conversation before Charlotte went into the kitchen, returning with a large knife, which she pressed into James' hand, remaining in the room while he went upstairs to commit the crime.

'At first, that was all there was; a sequence of events repeated over and over while I stood watching, unable to move or cry out, for by now I could no longer distinguish the modern surroundings — I seemed to have been drawn almost completely back into the past. The effect was so real that, at any moment, I expected them to look at me standing there, eavesdropping upon their conversation.

'Yet they gave no sign that they were aware of my presence. That was to come later — and in the most soul-destroying and horrible manner I could imagine.

'Only on one occasion did I witness an extension of the endlessly repetitive scene. The day had been sunny with an unaccustomed heat in the air for early April. I had taken my evening meal out in the garden and, for some unaccountable reason, had fallen asleep in the chair. It was several hours later when I woke, cold and stiff. The sun had set sometime earlier and it was now dark with the moon, nearing first quarter, slanting down towards the west.

'Rubbing my head groggily while trying to collect my thoughts, I suddenly had the feeling that something was wrong. At first I was unable to detect what it was, yet the sensation was so overpowering that I got abruptly to my feet, swaying slightly as cramp bit into the muscles of my legs.

'The grounds seemed to be different. There were bushes and trees where I knew they had no right to be. And the house —

'It, too, had changed dramatically. There was an air of newness about it, which sent a sudden chill through me. Lights were showing in several of the windows and, with a sudden shock of horror, I knew I was seeing it as it was two centuries earlier!

'As I watched, the lights began to go out, one by one, until only one remained in the upstairs window which I knew to be that of the room in which I slept. Finally, that too was extinguished and everything was in darkness. No sound broke the silence. It was as if the entire world were holding its breath, waiting for something to happen.

'Now the house was barely distinguishable from its background but then, after what seemed an interminable time, a light appeared. The front door had opened and a slim, dark figure appeared holding a lantern. Behind it was another shape, a grotesque outline, which, at first sight, appeared oddly inhuman. It was not until the two figures came out into the open that I realised that the second figure was a man carrying something bulky and heavy over his shoulders.

'Then, in a flash of understanding, I knew what I was witnessing. Charlotte Malmesly lighting the way for her lover as he carried the ungainly corpse of her husband to his final resting place in a shallow grave among the trees! The two shapes moved away into the dark anonymity of the wood and I was left, shivering uncontrollably, staring after them. It was not until that moment that the realisation came to me that, in all the time I had been witness to this ghastly succession of events, I had never once encountered the spirit of William Malmesly; had never, as far as I was aware, heard his voice among those eerie whispers.

'Turning, I made to pick up my chair and carry it back into the house, only to find, to my utter consternation, it was no longer there. What had happened? Was it possible that all of this had had a greater effect upon my nerves than I had imagined? Had I somehow taken the chair inside, yet remembered nothing of it?

'My nerves fretting, I stumbled towards the door and went inside, into a chill darkness. Strangely frightened, I entered the front room, looked around for the table with my typewriter on it, striving to pick out details in the faint moonlight which filtered through the windows with the heavy drapes on either side and —

'But there had been no drapes at the windows! In disbelieving horror, I stared at the massive oak table, which extended almost a full length of the room, at the dimly-visible portraits on the walls. Everything had changed. This was not the furniture, nor the room, I had known for three months.

'Staggering towards the stairs, aware that something was dreadfully wrong, I mounted them slowly. Was I dreaming? Halfway up the wide stairway was a full-length mirror, which I could not remember seeing before. Glancing into it as I passed, I suddenly swayed as utter shock tore through my mind, clutching at the wide banister for support. That reflection in the glass; the image of a man already past middle age with broad, florid features and dressed in a white shirt, knee breeches and hose . . .

'It was impossible! This couldn't be happening! If I was not mad, this entire uncanny business could only mean that, by some devilish means, I had been projected back into the past, back into the body of William Malmesly!

'I do not know how it is — how this insanity has come upon me. After seeing the grotesque reflection in the mirror, I somehow reached my room but even that was changed. The modern bed on which I had slept every night for months was now a huge four-poster with stiff linen sheets. Unable to think clearly I undressed, flinging the familiar clothing onto the floor. If I was somehow in the middle of a nightmare I told myself it would be gone by the morning and I would wake to find myself back in my normal bed, in the normal world.

'Somehow, despite the riot of thoughts which raced chaotically through my bemused mind, I fell asleep. When I woke, I was still permeated with the utter horror of the previous night, unable to force my thoughts back into normal channels. My entire body felt strange and there was an ache in my limbs, which had never previously been there. With an effort, I got out of bed and moved to the window. It was daylight outside and in the pale grey light of dawn I saw, to my horror, that the grounds were not the same as those with which I was familiar. There was a wide lawn, bordered by neat flowerbeds with narrow stone paths between them.

'I knew then that the hallucination had not passed; that I was enmeshed within an insanity of utter horror and sleep had not taken away the madness with which I was seemingly afflicted. By some terrible twist of fate — or was it some diabolical machination on the part of the long-dead William Malmesly — I was no longer in the year 1982 but trapped in the body of a man doomed to be murdered sometime in the middle of the eighteenth century!

'Now I have decided to write down a full account of all that has happened. Not that it will help me, in any way, to avert the horror which is to come, but I am anxious to make some record of these hideous and unbelievable events. I can only write at intervals for these pages must be seen by no one around. The servants have, inevitably, noticed a change in the person they believe is their master. I have heard them muttering among themselves in the kitchen, falling silent when they become aware of my presence.

'Charlotte watches me like a hawk as if she suspects something to which she cannot put a name. Each night, I fall asleep hoping when I wake in the morning I will find myself back in my own body and that this is only a dream, but each dawn brings the increasing horror of knowing that this will never happen, but I must live out whatever few days are left to me until that ineluctable night when there will be footsteps in the corridor outside my room; and the door will burst open and that black-hearted villain will break in and this time, unlike the earlier vision, the knife and the hand which wields it will be real!

THE END

We do hope that you have enjoyed reading this large print book.

Did you know that all of our titles are available for purchase?

We publish a wide range of high quality large print books including:
Romances, Mysteries, Classics
General Fiction
Non Fiction and Westerns

Special interest titles available in large print are:
The Little Oxford Dictionary
Music Book, Song Book
Hymn Book, Service Book

Also available from us courtesy of Oxford University Press:
Young Readers' Dictionary
(large print edition)
Young Readers' Thesaurus
(large print edition)

For further information or a free brochure, please contact us at:
Ulverscroft Large Print Books Ltd.,
The Green, Bradgate Road, Anstey,
Leicester, LE7 7FU, England.
Tel: (00 44) 0116 236 4325
Fax: (00 44) 0116 234 0205

Other titles in the
Linford Mystery Library:

THE ROYAL FLUSH MURDERS

Gerald Verner

Superintendent Budd is called in by the local police of Long Millford to investigate the strange murder of John Brockwell, impaled to the trunk of a tree with a pitchfork. Pinned to the lapel of the dead man's jacket is a playing card: the ten of diamonds. What is the meaning of this sign left on the body? Who hates the unpleasant Brockwell family so intensely, and why?